The Truth You Can't Betray

Cover Design by
Ayesha A. Chaney & Kurojintu.com

For booking information please send an email to traychaney@yahoo.com.

To order additional copies, please contact us.
BookSurge, LLC
www.booksurge.com
1-866-308-6235
orders@booksurge.com

TRAY CHANEY IN
COLLABORATION
WITH
YOLONDA D. COLEMAN

THE TRUTH YOU
CAN'T BETRAY

2006

The Truth You Can't Betray

This is a Coffeedreamz Experience.
Dream. Sip. Create.
www.coffeedreamz.com

In Loving Memory Of
Grandma Omega E. Chaney
Eric L. Hayes, II

FORWARD

In life you'll meet those who talk about plans and those who see those plans through. Tray Chaney not only creates blueprints for his future, but he also makes sure those plans are manifested into tangible evidence of his behind the scenes work. Tray's track record bleeds perseverance, determination and drive. When he seems to be derailed, Tray starts building new tracks and keeps on moving.

The Truth You Can't BeTRAY strays away from the biography that just talks about the woes and struggles of an acclaimed celebrity. We're going to show you rather than tell you the life adventures that brought Tray Chaney to his growing success.

Tray has a past that even on a good day he can't put it aside. We either learn from life's lessons or we are broken by them. With that said we must make better decisions or accept the consequences that result from our choices.

As Tray's story unfolded, I was even skeptical. "Nah Ahn...this ain't happen to you," I kept saying as I worked with Tray. I found myself in a zone where grammar didn't matter. Time was the truth serum that allowed me to see Tray's past in the present. I unknowingly met many of the interesting people mentioned in *The Truth.* In my research, I came across clips of Tray dancing his heart out on the stage of the Lincoln Theater. I'm still amazed at how quickly his legs moved to the beat. During one of our meetings, I was blessed to enjoy one of Mama

Chaney's fried chicken dinners. Campbell's has nothing on her. Dinner was "MMM MMM Good." The defining moment for me was reading a news clips about a very emotional time Tray endured. Regardless of the cause, the effect affected me years later.

Having spent quite a bit of time with the Chaney family, I've done my best to capture the true spirits of these very real, down to earth family members. There is a lot of love in the Chaney house. You too will pull up a chair in your literary mind to have dinner with Elaine and Skip, Tray's parents. You will become a cousin sitting in the living room eating barbecue meatballs and string beans as *The Wire* premiers on HBO. You might even find yourself fussing at Tray when you read about some of the crazy situations he placed himself.

Since you don't have time to waste, we're going to make each page count. If you're not laughing, angry or filled with anticipation, I'll give you a bus token for a wasted trip to the store (Okay, maybe not). Seriously, don't take my word for it. Flip the page and enjoy the ride.

Yolonda D. Coleman
Coffeedreamz Ink, LLC

A MOTHER'S NOTE: MY DANCING BABY
by Elaine Chaney

Tray was always dancing. Even when he was a little baby he would bounce as soon as he heard music. At the age of 4, he would make up his own routines. And in the 2nd grade, there was a talent show at Glenridge Elementary School in Landover Hills, MD. My baby crashed through the door so fast after school that he almost broke the thing down. He wanted to do his Bobby Brown routine to *My Prerogative* for the show. He had that down pat.

"Baby, you sure you wanna do this by yourself," I asked him. A resounding "Yes!" came from his mouth. Tray had a little body but his spirit was big.

I dabbled in sewing and committed to get my baby ready for his performance. I made him a pair of ivory, baggy pants and a suit jacket. He wanted to look just like Bobby. My baby was ready to take the stage.

Out of twenty-five kids to perform Tray won first place. The family and I cheered and screamed and just went crazy. Then his Uncle Jimmy had an idea.

"Why don't we take Tray to the Apollo in New York? I'm sure he could win," Jimmy suggested.

What did we have to lose? Nothing. Skip, my husband, and I left the arrangements in Jimmy's hands. A year or so later, Jimmy connected Tray with Ms. Jane Harley.

Ms. Harley coordinated local talent shows for performers in the D.C. area. Selected performers would be bussed to New York City to perform at the Apollo. She set up an audition for Tray at the Blackburn Center on Howard University's campus. After Tray's audition with

Ms. Harley and her staff, they all had the same response. "He's so small! Are you sure he'll dance in front of all those people in New York and not be scared?"

I held my head up high in confidence and said, "My baby is not shy."

SEASON ONE EPISODE ONE
Rubbing the Log

One Five Double OH! Fifteen hundred! That was the number of screaming people in the audience. 'Bout ten percent of them were my family and friends. Now, I'm no Luther Vandross, but I was the Superstar that night behind the stage. Me, Samuel "Tray" Chaney---the third of my kind in the family. Even though I was only 8, I wasn't nervous.

Sixty seconds stood between me and a lucky log. I was about to step onto the stage at the world famous Apollo Theater. The five boroughs of New York City and pieces of my hometown, PG County and Washington, D.C., would soon be my target. I remember that day as if I had the DVD of my life on constant rewind.

"Booooooo! The all too familiar sound of displeased audience members filled the air. It was a signal for some of the first acts to get off the stage. There was one more performance before I made my debut. Even with the possibility of being booed, I was too hyped---better yet, that was the dance group just before me. They didn't get booed. They set the joint on fire. The atmosphere was blazing. They later went on to dance back up for Ralph Tresvant during his solo career---after New Edition's NE Heartbreak success.

The next thing I knew Ralph Cooper, the legendary host of Apollo's Amateur Night, welcomed me onto the stage. "Aaaw he's so cute" came from several people as I tried to adjust to the bright lights blinding my little eyes. Then the cheers from my crew were in the air.

"TRAAAAAAAAAAAAAAAAY! WE LOVE YOU TRAAAAAAAAAAAAAY!" I heard a combination of high-pitched screams and drum bass voices in the audience. Mom shook in excitement with her hair staying in place. It was pulled back into a shiny French roll. As cool as a fan, Dad cheered for me as if I was his favorite group from the 70s. He was sharp in his dress slacks, brown blazer and striped shirt with the top button open. Dad gave me the thumbs up. I felt the energy of everyone looking---it made my body shake. Even before the music started, I was ready to blow up the spot. I took my cue. The music started. In that minute, on December 9, 1989, a star was born.

The echo of a man's voice boosted from the sound system. It was from Rob Base and DJ E-Z Rock's "It Takes Two." It was OVER! Each move, each gyration and split after the intro sent the audience into an eruption of cheers. They shouted, "Go Tray! Go Tray!" I was amped.

If Bobby Brown and MC Hammer did it in their videos, I mastered the moves with my additives. I was now using them to amaze the audience.

When my three-minute routine ended, I felt like I'd died and gone to heaven. I looked down at the stage and saw that it was littered with dollar bills ranging from singles to twenties. It was unreal. It only got better when I noticed one man, who was draped in a huge gold chain and a mink coat wave me towards the balcony. He dropped a one hundred dollar bill my way. It was rap's original lady's man, The Kane---Big Daddy Kane.

I collected my money and moved off the stage feeling like the luckiest kid in the world. Just being in the spotlight at the Apollo was big enough, but to get so much love on my first go was unbelievable.

My Uncle Jimmy stood behind the stage with huge eyes and mouth held open wider than a Skins fan after an interception. My pace was quick and slow at the same time. I was moving, but the air wasn't. Uncle Jimmy grabbed me and gave me an enormous hug.

"Tray," Uncle Jimmy shouted, "Tray, man, you tore it up! I can't believe it!"

My Kool-Aid smile took over as Uncle Jimmy kept me close to him.

I was rushed by familiar and unfamiliar faces. I remember looking around and seeing Mike Tyson. Then a young, talent representative approached Uncle Jimmy about me dancing in a video for one of his rappers, Father MC. That talent rep was P. Diddy---Sean Combs then.

Time was the bodyguard that kept us from shaking hands and rubbing elbows with all those who wanted to meet us. It was time to go back out on stage for them to announce the winning act. The ten acts filed in a single line facing the audience. I was in the middle.

I had my eye on another lady who was sitting on the front row. She scared me with that wild lookin' Jheri Curl. I was afraid she was going to run onto the stage, grab me and get some of that curl drip on the fresh outfit that Mom made for me.

The Apollo model walked behind each act and placed her hand above our heads. It was time for the audience vote---clap or boo was the method of voting. I focused in on my Mom and Dad. I managed to find them among the screaming and jumping people in the audience.

"Skip, that's our baby!" I imagined Mom saying as she waved at me and spoke to Dad at the same time. At that moment, winning didn't matter. The prideful look on Dad's face was enough for me. I smiled and Mom and Dad smiled back.

Before too long, the rest of the crowd rose to their feet in applause. I looked up at the model. Her hand was above my head. It was by far the loudest the audience had clapped. With four more acts to go one thing was clear, I was in the lead. The verdict held until I was announced the winner.

My parents, family and friends were all so proud of me. I think I smiled so much that my cheeks must have ached for a week. Man, when I arrived home it was like one big block party. More aunts, uncles, cousins and friends were waiting for me with hugs. I felt like a celebrity. But don't get it twisted, my parents kept me well grounded so this round head of mine wasn't allowed to get big.

Practical people, Mom and Dad raised my sister Candis and me the same way. We were taught that you didn't brag about what you had. "You ain't sposed to get too big for your britches," they would say. Although I knew the value of the money that I had collected from the Apollo, I also knew the values my family instilled in me.

It was "Showtime!" The episode with me on it was airing, so Grandma Rosa invited us over to watch it. We sat around the TV like it was going out of style. When I appeared, the house was in an uproar. Candis' silly butt looked like a Mexican jumping bean. She was all over the place screaming, "It's Tray! It's Tray!" Me---I felt strange looking at myself on television. I still couldn't believe it. Even though I won, I critiqued every step and every move. I knew that I could do better the next time.

Proud, Candis became my first publicist. At 4, she was telling more people before I had the chance to get to them. Only a few of my close buddies knew about my performance. Candis, with her bouncing ponytails, big round eyes and bubbly personality, made sure that was short lived. "My brother this, my brother that," came out of her mouth everywhere we went. I became really popular in my school 'cause word had spread throughout the neighborhood. The older kids pointed and the younger ones whispered.

Kids came up to me and asked, "Hey ain't chu that boy that be dancin' on tha Apollo?" After I said yes, they wanted me to dance right there in the hallway of the school.

"Do sumpthin', shortay! Do sumpthin'!"

The response was so great that I was invited back to the Apollo four more times and I won four more times. When it was all over I was left with a wealth of exposure to a world I'd never really planned to enter. It made me hungry 'cause I had the desire to do it all again.

Since Uncle Jimmy was responsible for getting me started at the Apollo, I looked to him for guidance.

"So what we gone do now?" I asked Uncle Jimmy.

"I'm not sure. It's really up to your parents," he replied.

I wasn't sure what my parents would say. They were excited about my success, but they would have some serious reservations about me being in show business. A few talent shows were fine, but pursuing entertainment as a career was something all together different. As much as I could control the moves I made on stage, my parent's thoughts I could not. I was still "just a kid."

There's nothing like a parent to keep you grounded. Dad always had to keep things in perspective. Don't get me wrong, he's the coolest father anyone could have, but don't let his smile fool you. Even with a grin wider than the Potomac River, Dad is a no nonsense kinda guy.

Flat out, Dad said that if I didn't keep my priorities in order---school, taking care of house chores, and most importantly, honoring Jehovah (not Jay-Z for those young cats out there), that he would put a stop to whatever extracurricular activities I had brewing. It was as simple as that.

I guess by now you're picturing me in a three piece suit on a Saturday knocking on your door to "witness." My parents have been devout Jehovah's Witnesses for as long as I could remember. Each and every Sunday and even a couple of times during the week, you'd catch my family and I at The Hall. It's what was expected. Like I said, Dad kept things in perspective. No Jehovah. No play.

I got away with not doing my chores around the house sometimes. I was on television and had won money for performing on the show. A thousand bucks a show plus the money that was thrown from the stands, I was sitting pretty. How many third graders had five grand collecting dust in their bank accounts? It was unbelievable. But Dad didn't care one way or the other. If I didn't do what was right, I'd end up feeling like five pennies when he got through with me.

Trying to be slick, I started spending the night at Uncle Jimmy's every weekend. I didn't feel like being bothered with anything to do with home, especially chores, going to the Kingdom Hall or anything that didn't lead me on a stage.

Uncle Jimmy was focused on my career. So he had 100 percent of my trust. Then it happened.

One Sunday after I came from Uncle Jimmy's spot, Dad sat in the living room waiting for me. He was short on words. It was cool at first since I was already tired from performing at a local mall the day before.

After I got comfortable in my room, Dad came in and closed the door behind him. I remember thinking, *"Boy, I'm in trouble!"* But in a calm voice, he spoke with me. It was like advice or something like a *for-your-own-good-father-knows-best* type thing. Not understanding or maybe not wanting to understand, I listened as the words parted his lips.

"Tray, it's real simple. Yeah, you can dance. You've got
a gift. But right now you're too young to know how to
handle being in the business. Show business is not a place
where people put Jehovah first. How you gonna do a show on
Saturday, stay up late and then miss the meeting on Sunday?
It's not happening. You're gettin' caught up in all the
Excitement." Dad said his peace.

I remember the speech like it was yesterday. Hit me right here (pounding my chest). As heavy as my heart was, I was trying to understand what he was saying, but I didn't want to believe what I thought I was hearing. My career was coming to an end before it even got started. I was waiting for Dad to say "siiiike" or something. It's like he fed me a choke sandwich and no milk. What was that all about?

"So, you sayin' I can't go to Uncle Jimmy's no more?"

I managed to say. With no emotion, he replied, "I'm saying me and your mother agree that you're gonna have to put your dancing on hold for a while."

STOP PLAYING, DAD! I wanted to shout, but continued to wonder how he could crush my dreams so easily. I won't ever say that I hated my dad, but at that very second...that one moment in time...hmm...I did not like him very much (that's putting it mildly---my bad Dad. In fact, I almost wished that Uncle Jimmy was my dad. This was a point where Dad lost his cool.

As a tear began to form in the corner of my eyes, I pleaded beginning with the famous whine, *But Daaaaaaad!* He cut me off without hesitation. It was like he read my mind when he said shouted, "Jimmy is not your father! Somewhere you lost track of that, son. If you wind up going down the wrong path it's on me and Elaine. That's not going to happen while I'm alive. No sir. Not on my watch!"

Try Again Next Time invisibly panned across Dad's face with his eyebrows flexed. He wasn't buying it.

"Even if you go to the Kingdom Hall, your mind won't be on what you're supposed to be learning. You'll be thinking 'bout the show you just performed or the next performance, Tray," Dad said.

All I could do was look at him with contempt in my little eyes. Before I could plead my case any further, which I was prepared to do, he added "Sorry son but that's just the way it is."

Dad's words would play over and over in my head for some time. My father turned the knob and walked out. Bam! The door of my future was closed. When he left I couldn't lock the door fast enough. I was now in cell block number three.

I didn't want Dad, Mom or Candis coming in my room to bother me. My only wish was that when I turned the knob to the door, I would magically be in Uncle Jimmy's house. If only there was a commercial break in my reality show, I would be there when we came back.

Lights! Camera! Action! I had the itch. I was quiet for six years, but when the show business bug hits you, there's nothing you can do but yield to it. My dream of being in front of the camera was reoccurring. Six years after *The Talk* with Dad, the desire to perform was stronger than ever. He was standing on his mission to ruin my life---so it seemed. I'm a performer. That's what I do. Thank God for mothers.

Mom later convinced Dad that one or two performances wouldn't hurt. Permission was granted. By the time I got to high school, all kinds of opportunities were available to me. Some opportunities were good and some were not so good. If it was before me, I was on it. There weren't as many lights as I expected, but there was plenty of action!

My freshmen year of high school was cool. My fuzz was coming in and I had a little weight on me. However, it was then that I was introduced to, or more accurately, inherited the Swann Road and Regency Meadows ongoing feud. These were neighborhoods in Forestville, MD.

Back in the day, we had crews not gangs. The battle between Swann Road and Regency Meadows had been going on for years. The tripped out part about it was no one knows how it all got started. One thing was for sure, many lives had been affected by it. I tried to stay out of this brawl, but 'cause I resided in Regency Meadows, it was no getting around it. So either I was going to be on guard and ready, run from it--- which wasn't going to happen---or be an innocent victim of it. As I was told earlier by one of the Swann Road guys, "Either you do what you have to do or you die." I had big plans, but dying young wasn't one of them.

I wasn't used to fighting for my life, but what was the alternative? I couldn't sleep at night thinking about what I would get into the next day at school. I was always angry 'cause of the fighting that I had to do while in school. I never smiled on any of my school pictures 'cause it was not a happy time for me.

"Baby, why don't you smile in your pictures?" Mom would ask.

"Ain't nuthin' to smile about," I replied.

Every time I heard the name Swann Road, I got this terrible feeling in my stomach and started muggin' 'cause their energy was just so evil. I even thought about getting a gun just in case they tried to jump me. I didn't, but the thought was always on my mind.

It was nothing for students to bring a hammer to school. It had become a part of the school culture. Tension was thick most of the time. There had been shootings and stabbings in and around the school like a scheduled lunch or homeroom. Everyone was up on their game.

I always had to be on guard at school. It was no place to learn to read and write anymore. It felt more like a jail full of hard core criminals that would kill you if you didn't watch your back. Just standing in the hall was cold and scary. I never wanted to walk the halls alone---not even to go to the restroom. When I did go alone, I had to do my business and get out of there before someone came in the bathroom and noticed I was by myself.

People would give you a dirty look from the time you arrived to school until the time you left to go home. You always had to worry about others jumping in and beating you practically to death. People don't fight fair anymore these days, so people would feel the need to bring weapons for that person who was beating them on the head along with his friends. Once everyone knew that you had your weapon, they would know better than to mess with you. So the weapons were bought to school for protection only.

Forest Creek, another nearby crew, was beefing with some people around the way. Forest Creek was known for its share of violence in PG County. Guns, knives, and weed were heavy on the block and as the opportunity presented itself, I was right there. I was in the dirt contrary to what my parents wanted.

My first time smoking was just supposed to be an ordinary experience. But Naaaah, somebody got me and got me good. I knew right from wrong, but I figured it couldn't be that bad. Plus, no one, especially my parents, had to know about it. I was at school and I would be okay by the time I got home. Right? Hee! Hee! Sniff. I was wrong!

My buddies thought it was funny to give me a laced blunt. To this day I have no clue what was swimming in my spliff. To be honest, I don't want to know nor do I ever want anymore of that stuff. Talk about tripping out! I was on vacation. Anyway, I didn't want anything laced but my lady in the bedroom. I was in such bad shape that Mom had to pick me up from school. That wasn't supposed to be a part of the plan.

The school called Mom and told her that my heart was racing. When she arrived at the school, I was in a room with my head down. My eyes were lifted to partially acknowledge Mom's presence. The look on the principal's face and two other teachers were nothing compared to the one on my mother's grill. Mom looked beautiful on the surface, but beyond the bright, red lip stick I know her spirit was dim. She had the look of fury on her face and my heart dropped 'cause I felt so bad that I put myself in to this situation.

My mother was told that I had been smoking weed on school property. I'm sure the administration was ready for the "Not my child speech." On cue, Mom firmly stated that her son does not use drugs. Not wanting to believe what the authorities had told her and definitely not wanting to be embarrassed, she asked if she could have a moment alone with me.

Elaine Chaney broke me down. "Tray, have you been using drugs?"

I adamantly denied my use. Until I choked out the word "yes" after seeing her eyes say *Boy, you better not lie to me!*

On that note, she apologized to the principal and the teachers. Mom's French roll was tighter than ever. The buttons on her suit jacket were about to pop open and bust me in the face. She was heated. This wasn't a medical emergency, but I could hear the sirens ringing. I broke her heart and mine was broken for hurting her. Sorry, Mom.

By tenth grade it was on. The girls were on me. I had my first sexual encounter. Woo Hoo! I got caught up for real. Ironically, my girl lived on Swann Road, so I had to exploit the relationship. I was kicking it with one of the girls from enemy territory.

My family didn't care too much for her, but they were polite when she came around. It was during this time that I learned another valuable life lesson. Dirt done in the dark will come to light. My sneaking around *doing it* caused further distance between my father and me when it was discovered that my girl was pregnant. He was disgusted with me 'cause I embarrassed him. Being a Jehovah's Witness, it is the head of the household who is responsible for all that goes on in it. Since I was still under his care, he took it personal and this was shared with the Elders at the Kingdom Hall.

When all was said and done, I was on reproof or limited restrictions at The Hall. Later, we found that the girl "lost the baby." As if things couldn't get any worst, it was on a regular that fights were breaking out and I was being approached, taunted and threatened. Staying at Uncle Jimmy's wasn't a bad idea after all, huh Dad?

By eleventh grade, I felt there was no way out. I kept all that I was going through to myself. I didn't want Mom to worry like most mothers would. I was so caught up that I didn't even realize how much it was taking a toll on my life. At school I was fighting a turf war with the rival gang. At home I was fighting a losing battle.

My bitterness for my father was due to his quiet animosity towards me and his overly-affectionate manner toward my sister. She was cute, but dag! I had real problems that needed attention.

I also had an internal struggle. I still wanted to perform but I didn't want to appear corny to my new audience, my crew. A dancing thug? Be for real! I couldn't justify it. My boys would have laughed me out. I was confused, trapped and mad at the world.

By senior year, I had come to make some decisions about my life after hearing about dudes dropping like flies. They were dying young. I didn't want the same for myself. My parents didn't have any idea what was going on in my life since I kept to myself. That was a call for help. Silence ain't always golden. Mom and Dad should have listened to mine.

As far as Mom and Dad were concerned, I was an honor roll student and maintained my B average throughout high school. With the exception of my Marion Barry moment of getting caught smoked out, there was no need to be too concerned about their son. At this point in my life, it didn't matter to me

COMMERCIAL BREAK
On The Inside Looking Out

The mind is a funny thing. You can feel like you're on top of the world one moment, but a subtle reminder can take you into another space, another place or another time in your life. Every so often that reminder can be a pleasant get away. Other times, those memories can be hard to revisit.

When you're healthy, you have the world in front of you. When your health is failing, you have a world of concerns around you. My dad knows all too well how unfavorable news from a doctor can change your entire being.

It was an ordinary evening when everyone in my family came home from work or school. The hugs and *how was your day dialogue* were normal as we each made our way to our rooms to get ready for our weekly Bible meeting. Mom and Dad were in their room and suddenly I heard Mom say in a raspy and concerned voice, "Skip, what happened?"

I wasn't sure whether to walk in their bedroom or just stand at the door and listen with a glass up to it. Seeing that I didn't have a glass I decided to knock on the door.

Tap! Tap! "Ma?"

"Tray?" she asked with heaviness in her throat.

"Yeah, it's me. Can I come in?"

Mom dragged her feet across the floor in what sound like bedroom slippers and opened the door. Creeeek! The door was squeaking at the hinges preparing me for the unexpected.

On the edge of the bed sat Dad. Nothing unusual, right? That was until I noticed his pants around his ankle. Mom was fully dressed and Teddy P wasn't singing in the background.

Dad had his head down. He was looking away with sad eyes. Those were clear signs that I hadn't walked in on anything freaky.

My face was wrinkled with worry. I never expected to catch

Dad with his pants down. He sat there and I saw myself years down the road. We shared so many features in common---round head, round eyes, dark hair. When I looked closer, his legs were smaller than mine. This scared me.

"Dad! What's going on?" I asked.

"Son, I don't know." Dad threw his hands in the air. "I tried to put my suit on and my pants just fell right off."

I looked at Dad's exposed legs. He had lost a noticeable amount of weight. He was already small in frame but this was unlike any other weight loss, mostly 'cause he wasn't trying.

"I need to see a doctor," Dad confirmed. Then he looked down at himself and then back at Mom. Vibes and intuition can tell you more than spoken words. Needless to say, we didn't make it to the Kingdom Hall that night.

Without hesitation Mom got on the telephone to call Dr. Gokuland, our family doctor. We had an appointment set for 9 the next morning. Mom and Dad were there ahead of time.

Dr. Gokuland ran a series of tests on Dad then told him to go home and get some rest. The good doctor informed my parents that he would be calling them in a few days with the results. Patience really is a virtue 'cause those few days felt like eternity.

Hardheaded, Dad didn't follow the doctor's orders to a tee. Day two after visiting Dr. Gokuland, guess who was back at work on his regular route at Fed X? That's right! Good ole Dad. In fact, he was at work when the doctor's office called to give the results. Thank God for cell phones.

"Skip, are you sitting down?" Mom called Dad on the job.

"If not, baby, please take a seat," she warned.

Mom continued to tell him that his test results came back. Dr. Gokuland said that Dad should not be at work 'cause his lungs could collapse. He has something called Sarcoidosis. Sarcoidosis, an incurable disease that causes an inflammation of various organs. The cause---unknown.

I wanted to know everything I could about the disease. How did it affect people? Was it deadly? Was it hereditary? Mom, Candis and I did more research. We found out that Sarcoidosis is not a form of cancer. That was a relief. It is not contagious. So we didn't have to quarantine Dad. We later discovered that Sarcoidosis could occur in almost any part of your body, although it usually affects some organs more than others. It usually starts in the lungs or the lymph nodes.

Dad's illness started in his lungs and he was put on a medication called Prednisone. It's a steroid he had to take for 6 months. This drug caused Dad to blow up to an unnoticeable weight. We went from one extreme to the next. He had never weighed more than 140 lbs. Dad gained 20 pounds in no time. People started poking fun at him without knowing he was sick. That aggravated me. Others thought Dad could stand to carry a few extra pounds 'cause he was a tad on the small side.

"You look good, Skip. I like that look on you," a random relative said.

Prednisone can also cause mood swings. My parents would go at it like nothing I'd ever heard. They were each other's first loves and were proud to admit that to anybody. So to hear them yelling at the top of their lungs at each other scared me. I thought Candis and I were going to be products of a split home.

After Dad's 6 months were up, the doctor took him off the medication. Dad's attitude changed back to the nice, calm loving husband that my mom married. He also loss the 20 pounds he gained. Welcome back, Skip!

The Sarcoidosis didn't leave him. The worse part of the disease had transferred itself from inside onto the external parts of his body. Although the sores were ugly, we were glad to know the disease had not started attacking any other major parts of his body like his liver or heart.

Dad has been living with Sarcoidosis for twenty-years now. No matter the disease, he still makes that trek to work in rain, sleet, snow or extreme heat. He occasionally gets a bump or two on his chest, but topical medication clears that up.

I think about this disease often and I worry about Dad more than normal. Mom continues to support her first love, and Candis and I help out whenever necessary. In his mid-forties, I know Dad is strong. I can't imagine my life without him. I pray each and every night that nothing tragic happens to him. So far my prayers have been answered.

Sarcoidosis is painful for the carrier, but it is also painful to watch a loved one suffer from it. If only a bandage and a kiss from Mom could take it away. If only...

*T*ray did a dance routine in front of me. I didn't think he could polish off, but he did it in a way...WHEW! (gets down on the floor and rises with his hands waving) I had never seen before. Candis can dance too. She just doesn't steal her brother's light. My boy can dance! He must have been practicing after I told him know back in the day. Who knew dancing would be the ticket for his success?

-Samuel "Skip" Chaney

my experimentation with the *ooh weed* worsened. I was outta school and didn't have jack to do. An idle mind truly is the *devil's workshop*. My parents were getting pissed off each and every day with me 'cause kickin' it on the couch watching B.E.T. was becoming the norm.

Mom and Dad would harp on me and ask "Why do you want to be a bum? Go out and get a job!" While they were at work during the day I was sneaking girls in and out the back door so the nosey neighbors wouldn't see me. *Gettin' mine* in the middle of the day was hard work.

With all of the negativity that I was bringing on myself, I was still going to the Kingdom Hall. I had a good heart, but sometimes I just didn't consider my spiritual obligations when it came to women and having fun. No one knew about my activities---nobody on earth anyway.

Although I lead a double life, I still took in positive advice. One Sunday after The Hall, a Brother by the name of Frank Pews asked my parents if he could spend some time with me to offer some words of encouragement. Apparently, my secret life was making public appearances. Little by little people were starting to see the negative slope I was headed towards. Grown folks would say, "What you do in the dark will come to light."

Frank took me to get something to eat. Amidst the clanking of forks and giggles of children around us, he shot from the hip.

"Tray, man, what do you want to do with your life? What is your passion? What makes you feel good other than coming to The Kingdom Hall?"

Pow! Pow! Pow! One question after the other hit me in the head. I didn't know where to begin. For real, I never really thought of answers to those questions in recent history 'cause

I didn't think anybody cared about what I wanted. So I went with what I knew best.

"I want to be in front of a lot of people." Bam! That was my answer---simple and plain. I just want to be an entertainer. I want to hear the applause! I want to be in lights! I want the girls screaming for me. I was all too familiar with grown folks saying "All that glitters ain't gold," but even if for a moment, I was prepared to live in the fantasy.

Frank laughed and said, "If that's all you want to do then go for it! You're older now. Start making some decisions for yourself." He was right. I was grown. Up 'til that point in my life, my parents had already brainwashed me to listen to whatever they wanted for me. What Tray wanted didn't matter. I was unhappy following the wishes of other people.

After Frank dropped me off at home, I sat in my room and started thinking of a way I could convince everyone in the family, including my parents that I was made for the stage, a set, the lights, the camera and all the action. I was born to be in the entertainment industry. I didn't know how it would happen, but I was going to keep working toward the goal to get back into show biz.

I came up with a plan. It was a Monday when I went out to look for jobs. Application after application was filled out. In order to get copies of my pictures, biography and resume done to circulate in the industry, I had to pay for it. The money had to come outta my pocket. Instead of making dough illegally, I worked for my cash. One of the jobs that I applied for was at JCPenney. Come to find out this dude named Lamont from The Hall was a manager there. By Friday I was hired.

The look of shock on my parents face was incredible. Mom's grin was stuck on pause. Dad kept giving me the universal strong man hug---pulled me close and patting my back real hard. I was a working man. I had a 9 to 5 for the first time in my life.

I saved my money for headshots so I could start submitting them to agencies, talent competitions and anywhere else that would help me reach my super star dreams.

I heard about a talent show at the Lincoln Theatre in D.C. sponsored by WKYS 93.9 FM, a local radio station. The morning drive announcer, Russ Parr, was hosting it. The auditions were from 6PM to 9PM. My shift didn't end until 5PM so I asked my supervisor if I could leave early 'cause I had an emergency. He gave me permission to pass go.

I rushed home and pulled out a tape with a Janet Jackson song on it. Even though I was using drugs, sexing women and being disobedient, I stayed true to my first love and continued to keep up with the latest dance moves and hottest music. I had to be ready just in case the opportunity to dance in front of a crowd presented itself.

I called Uncle Jimmy to take me to the audition. He was with it. It was time to turn up the heat and make new fans. He picked me up at 5PM and we headed to the Lincoln Theatre.

I apparently wasn't the only one prepared to shine on stage. The line was long. You couldn't see the entrance to any of the stores on U Street 'cause of the crowd. The homeless people hanging out in the alley next to Ben's Chili Bowl, a historical restaurant next to the Lincoln Theater, had to make room. I guess that was to be expected since the event was advertised big time on the radio. Even with the $20 registration fee, starving artists were ready to make their moment on stage count.

We had to be gone in sixty seconds. The judges had one minute to decide our fate. When it was my turn, I was given a microphone and instructed to start singing.

"Uh, I don't sing or rap," I said with an innocent look on my face.

"Well what do you do, son?" a lady with a friendly but firm voice asked.

"Ma'am, I'm a dancer," I replied.

"Dancer?" another judge asked while the others looked in surprise.

"A Dancer," I confirmed with confidence.

Then with a little more composure, the lady said, "Then let's see you dance".

I handed her the tape and when the music started it was as if my feet had a mind all their own. The stage was my world. In that moment, I danced circles around time.

The lady stopped the tape and without cracking a smile said, "Thanks. We'll call you in a week." I left not knowing what to expect. When I got home, the phone rang and Dad answered.

"Stop kiddin' me," Dad kept saying.

When I walked in the kitchen Dad had the joker grin plastered all over his face as he handed me the phone.

"It's some guy named Carl saying you're in a talent show next month."

I anxiously grabbed the phone. Carl called to tell me to get ready to compete for a trip to New York and $1,000. That was the grand prize of $1,000. I didn't even hear what he said the second and third place prizes were 'cause I wanted to be #1. I had been in that spot before and was ready to get it back.

The night of the show was a major highlight. My family and friends gladly paid their $10 to get into the Lincoln Theatre. One dude wooed the audience with a nice selection on his saxophone. The ladies loved him. Then there was an older lady giving it her best shot with a Diana Ross song.

Then it was my turn. It had been almost ten years since I had performed for a huge Apollo style crowd. I was ready to shut it down. I felt the music and my body moved as I began to cut my puppet strings of life. My desire couldn't be controlled by anyone else's hands.

The crowd was out of control with their loud claps and cheers. If there was anything else bigger than my smile that day, it must have left the building 'cause I was cheezing. The competition was tough that night, but the greatest feeling was walking out of the Lincoln Theatre one thousand dollars richer. I was more excited than ever to go to the Big Apple, 'cause you know what some grown folks say, "If you can make it in New York City, you can make it anywhere."

SEASON ONE EPISODE FIVE
Fresh Fish on *The Wire*

I was a little fish trying to swim in a big pond. Linda Townsend knew that I had the potential to be a big fish who would create his own waters. Linda was courageous enough to become my manager. She discovered me, but had one concern. *Can you do anything else besides dance?*

I had completed a couple of drama classes in high school.

"I can act," I replied. Yet, I continued to express to her my desire to be a dancer.

"Tray, let's maximize your opportunities and focus on being an all around entertainer," Linda suggested.

I didn't argue, and we started submitting headshots to different casting agencies to see if I had what it took to be an actor.

Linda heard about a pilot being shot in Baltimore. The producers were pitching it to HBO. The casting call for *The Wire* was in the D.C., MD and Virginia areas. So, we took a stab at it and sent my information.

The casting agent called Linda and requested to see me in the Baltimore office. Just before the audition, I stopped by Linda's office to pick up the script. I wanted to memorize a few lines for a character named Wee Bey. I had never really acted before except in high school with the play *Either You Do or You Die*. So this was something that was kind of fresh for me.

When I arrived at the casting call, I saw a lot of dudes that had that same look of as I did---confident but nervous. We all had the lines for the character Wee Bey in our hands. As I looked around at my competition, I didn't think there was anything special that set me a part from the others.

"Why in the world did Linda set me up for this thing?" I mumbled to myself while looking over the script.

I was feeling a little discouraged 'cause I stood on unfamiliar territory. Yet, there I was preparing to make my way as an actor.

"Tray Chaney," a voice called my name. It was time to show them what I had or didn't have. I went in to face the firing squad with an I-don't-care attitude. Pat Moran, the casting director, looked as if she didn't care either.

I stated my name and the role in which I was auditioning. I was instructed that once she said "action", I was to start, and I went to work as soon as the words parted Pat's lips.

I had a two a two-minute window to read. Snap! Like that it was over. Pat sized me up for what seemed a slow motion eternity.

"Thanks," Pat said nonchalantly. I responded with a nod and walked out feeling like I had just wasted my time.

A week later, Linda called and said that Pat and the producers of the show wanted to see me. She was so excited on the phone, but I didn't share her enthusiasm. It was a call back and nothing more to me. Linda must have heard my half-hazard excitement over the phone.

"Tray, this is an HBO project! Why are you acting so, so uuuh?" Linda blurted out with curiosity.

"I don't know anything about the acting business. I'm saying, Linda. Do you really think they're going to pick me over someone who has more experience?"

Linda went on to explain to me that it is different from just being a dancer. If selected, I'd have more opportunities to be in the limelight. She knew the right buzz words to get me on board. That's what I wanted, so I was with going back to read for these producers and directors again. This time, I would have a new attitude.

Good ole Pat was front and center. She, along with the other executives gave me the same Wild West showdown stairs. All that was missing was the chewing tobacco and straw dangling from their lips. A feeling of uncertainty invaded my body. I walked in more confident, but walked out wishing I had stayed home to watch re-run episodes of Good times.

Strangely enough, I did return home only to start imagining what it would be like to appear on an HBO series. Then I remembered all the other callbacks sitting in the waiting room. I stopped dreaming 'cause I didn't have a chance.

A few weeks went by and the audition had almost slipped my mind. I was busy working and by the time I would get off of work, if I didn't have to go to The Hall, I was kicking it with my cousin Chicago and my friends Eric and Zeek. We just did what dudes do. Our time was spent hollering at the ladies, party hop, and just...acting a fool!

One Friday night, we were at Applebee's, just chillin', when my phone rang. It was Linda Townsend.

"Tray, you did it!" She was hysterical.

Somewhat baffled I managed to ask, "Did what?"

"You landed a role on *The Wire*. I mean you didn't get Wee Bey, but the executives liked you so much they created a character called Poot just for you."

"Are you serious?" My mouth was wide open with surprise.

"Yes! Poot is going to be featured in the HBO pilot." Linda further explained.

Hassan Johnson was cast as *Wee Bey*. That was cool, 'cause he has a load of experience. Hassan was seen in *Belly* with DMX and Nas, *In Too Deep* with Omar Epps and LL Cool J, Spike Lee's *Clockers* with Mekhi Phifer, Pedro Starr from the hip hop group Onyx and Isaiah Washington and a list of other films and TV shows. My man was doing his thing.

It had not been confirmed whether the show would get picked up. However, the opportunity was still priceless. My mind was flooded with running thoughts, but nothing was coming out of my mouth.

"Tray, you'll have to go to Baltimore to get fitted for your wardrobe," a frantic Linda said swiftly.

Tray Chaney was getting measured for a wardrobe? That was bananas. Linda also told me that I had to shave all my facial hair to give off the look of a fifteen-year-old. No problem! It was the least I could do for my career. Right?

My eavesdropping boys were anxious to know what the deal was.

"Man, you must have some good news!" Eric said.

"Ya'll ain't gonna believe this!" I told the fellaz that I was called to shoot a pilot for an HBO joint.

Eric was just as excited as I was. Chicago and Zeek joined in on the excitement. It was really time to celebrate.

Muffled sounds of congratulatory remarks circled the air as I tried to truly soak in all that I heard. Onlookers tried their best to find out what we were celebrating while trying to remain discrete. Chicago helped them out.

"YO! My man gonna be on HBO!" Chicago shouted and held up his glass in the Applebee's. A number of hand claps and an *ooh, it's nice to see young folks doing positive* thangz came from an elderly lady.

As I barely listened to the crowd since I was still trippin' that the show was being considered for a pilot run. Once we shot an episode we would still have to pitch it to the HBO network. In other words, this didn't mean it was a definite go ahead as far as it being on TV and all. Nonetheless, I had come a lot further than I thought when I went in to audition.

The rest of evening was spent joking about all the women we were going to get with my celebrity status. When Tray was in the crew was in, hence the "we" reference. You know the moment a honey saw you on television they automatically start daydreaming about the paper you were making. Nobody said anything about payment, yet, but I would be playing the role to see how far it would get me.

When I arrived home, my mom and dad were still sitting up in the kitchen during their thing ... entertaining each other with Some oldies but goodies and some drinks. Mom was drinking her favorite, red wine and dad was buzzed off his gin and juice. One more swallow, my parents would be on reprove. They were having a good time.

I sat down and announced that I had some crazy news. With their eyes glued on me, I could tell from the looks on their faces that they didn't know what to expect. I played right into it by not breaking a smile or a bead of sweat.

"Do you remember that HBO series I read for?"

Before I could finish my sentence, my mother let out a sigh of relief and my father had a silly-looking grin on his face as if to say, I'm so glad that this was not any bad news you were breaking to us. I continued to tell them about the role of Poot. With a sense of pride and smiles a mile long, they both congratulated me. My dad laughed like he always did and I felt good. It wasn't until I told him that I needed him to drive me to Baltimore to get fitted for the show that it really hit him. Yet it wasn't until I got on the set that it really hit me.

Without hesitation, Dad agreed to head north on I95 with me. The building for the wardrobe fitting was on Pratt Street in downtown Baltimore. Aside from the crime and abandoned buildings, Baltimore truly is a beautiful city. Like the D.C. area, the media gives it a bad rep.

On the way to the wardrobe fitting area, Dad expressed his pride for me. He hadn't done in a longtime. He said that he was not going to believe anything until he actually saw it with his own eyes. It was amazing to him that his son could possibly be on a nationally televised show one day. It would all be very real as soon as the receptionist buzzed us in.

Bzzz! Dad and I walked through the heavy doors with pride. On the other side were hair and make-up artists and a wardrobe crew just waiting to do their job. I felt like VEE EYE PEE! There was a photographer who was ready to aim and shoot at the direction of the crew. To my amazement, David Simon, the creator of *The Wire*, Executive Producer Robert Colesberry, and a lot of other VIPs who were at the second audition hanging around talking to each other. I was now in their world and they treated me and Dad like royalty.

Everyone was so nice and just unbelievably down to earth. This was the real deal! Colesberry handed me a script Along with a schedule for the first episode. Once everything Was completed at the office, we left. Dad talked about it all The way home.

"Son," Dad began. "I know I made decisions about your career you didn't like, but---"

I stopped him. "Dad, you don't even have to say anything."

"No! No! Listen son," he started while looking into the rear view mirror. "Even though you knew how I felt about you devoting time to the entertainment industry, you continued to follow your dreams. That took courage."

"You telling me?" I said jokingly knowing that I faced the *I told you so speech* if things didn't work out.

"It also showed me that you're coming into your manhood and being true to yourself." Dad hit my leg with his fist. "I'm proud of you."

Forget *Finding Nemo.* I was finding Tray, and I liked every bit of the direction he was headed. So here I was hooked on Life and everything it had to offer. I didn't want to sink. I Planned to swim like a shark, never turning back. Although *The Wire* wasn't a done deal for scheduling, it just felt right and So did I.

SEASON TWO EPISODE ONE
Embarking on the New Horizon

Exhilarating can't fully describe the feeling that I was experiencing on the first day I had when I first stepped on the set of *The Wire*. 6AM was reporting time. I was ready. I met with the hair and make-up staff. I was then shown to my trailer. What? That had to sink in. Tray Chaney had a trailer. HA! It was a portable apartment.

In the trailer was a couch, television, a refrigerator, a bathroom and a radio system. I wasn't in there for five minutes before someone knocked on the door.

"Mr. Chaney, what would you like for breakfast?" the lady in the khaki outfit asked. In comparison to home, this was paradise. I was just waiting for the next surprise to come out the closet---a babe wrapped in a towel ready to give me a massage. Wishful thinking never hurt anyone.

Right next to my trailer was a JD Williams. He starred in one of my favorite TV shows *OZ*. He played the character Kenny Wangler. Quiet as kept, he also had an appearance in Prince's *Graffiti Bridge*. I was officially star struck. I couldn't believe we'd be working on the same show. I had to get myself together 'cause I imagined, someday, some new kid was going to be on a set with me and I would have to be his mentor. My first words of advice to him would be, "get in where you fit in. Don't lose your cool even though you're amongst the stars." I hoped my overzealous behavior didn't scare my new co-workers away.

After coming out of dream world with all the amenities that Came along with my new job, I had to ready myself for the shoot. The first episode of *The Wire* went by with a breeze 'cause I didn't have any lines. However, I was in eight scenes with other key characters. Action! Cut! Take Seven! There were so many different takes. I know I did one scene thirty times. I had a new appreciation for actors. It's not as easy as the end product looks. I guess that's the beauty of acting, producing, directing, and editing. In the end, it all comes together. This was my training day.

We took lunch at noon. I can put food away, but I didn't even know where to start. The spread was straight: chicken, shrimp, fish, steak, desserts galore and plenty of drinks to wash it all down. The best part, I didn't have to touch my pockets.

While getting my grub on, I saw Wendell Pierce sitting in the lunchroom with me. He was Lela Rochon's overweight lover in *Waiting to Exhale*. Moments later, Idris Elba walked in to the eating area. He played the minister who took over a church in *The Gospel*---the one who thought he was bigger than the church. Then Wood Harris pops in to the joint. He is known for the role he played in *Above The Rim* with Tupac Shakur. I felt like a kid in a toy store with all his favorite games.

After lunch, I went back to my trailer to review my contract. I was getting a minimum of $750 per day. Sometimes, I would get a check for three grand per episode. I was impressed and soon realized I had to work even harder to maintain what was to become my new lifestyle.

From sun up to sun down we worked. When it was a rap, the cast was told that there was a two-week window to see if HBO would pick up the show. That was the longest two weeks of my life. HBO picking up the show meant that I was moving into another realm of entertainment. The local talent show was one ambition, but to be seen nationally was something big. This gig would just be the beginning of a long list of ambitions I planned to accomplish. It was full speed ahead from this moment forward.

SEASON TWO EPISODE TWO
PARTY OVER HERE! ZZZZ!

The days dragged on while I watched the telephone like it was going out of style. About the fifth day of my two week wait for the executives to call, I occupied my mind with other things. I put my total focus on my new 9 to 5 job at Melwood, an organization that offers employment and training for people with developmental disabilities. This job gave me a chance to work with and help people who are mentally and physically disabled. It was my way of doing something positive even though I was thuggin' on the set.

I was on break, one day, when I called home to check the voicemail. A lady named Nina left a message for me.

"Hi, this is Nina Noble. This message is for Tray Chaney.

The Wire has been picked up for thirteen episodes. Please give me a call so I can give you the shooting schedule."

Sniff! Sniff! Listening to that message brought tears to my eyes! Not 'cause I was sad, but 'cause I felt as though my dreams were coming into fruition. October 2001 will forever be engraved in my brain. It was the day I got "The Call."

I was expected to shoot for 7 months. I would have to break the news to my supervisor at Melwood. Although I loved my job, I wasn't willing to pass up this once in a lifetime opportunity. I mulled over my speech before speaking with Ron, my supervisor. Ron was a real cool guy to talk to and I had never given him any reason to doubt me. I sent him an email asking to speak with him about something really important.

I was kinda nervous. I figured if I told him about this big break he would automatically be like, *"Ok, Tray, so long and have a nice life."* I've heard of jobs letting you go when another opportunity conflicted with your regular 9 to 5 duties. They might consider you more of a liability than an asset.

Ron replied to my e-mail saying he was ready to talk whenever I was. I immediately made my way to his office. When I sat down I surprisingly felt at ease.

"Ron, I'm just going to be straight up. I love my job here, but I got a call from HBO. I've been cast for a new show called *The Wire."*

I confided in Ron that I had been in the entertainment business for some time before coming to Melwood. I also told Ron that I didn't want to lose my position at Melwood. I loved what the company did for the people they serve. I also offered to do commercials to help further its mission to employ and train the disabled.

Churp! Churp! Churp! Churp! I felt like I was in the woods 'cause the silence stood between us was thick. Ron starred at me for a moment. Then all of a sudden, a huge smile appeared on his face.

"Tray," Ron began. "You're a great worker and you can stay at Melwood as long as you need. I'm sure Melwood will support me on this decision 100 percent."

Whew! What a relief. That was much easier than I thought. The only thing Ron asked of me is that I give advance notice of my shooting schedule. They would place me on assignment accordingly. Ron's support and encouragement meant a lot. He made my day. As I left his office, I thanked him and my smile beamed across my face. Now, it was time to go home and share with the family.

I saved the message from Nina so my parents could hear it for themselves. I knew mom was going to straight trip---in a good way.

When I walked in the house, Dad was standing in the kitchen listening to the messages on the phone. He had a scowl on his face as if the bill collector was on the other end. BOMP! He pressed the delete button to skip the message. Out of the blue, Dad's facial expression went from serious to extremely surprised. I assumed he was checking out Nina's message by the Joker grin that formed. His smile got wider and wider.

"You did it, boy! You did it!" He almost sound like Mr. McDowell from "Coming to America" when he found out Akeem was a prince.

Dad kept pressing the button that allowed him to rewind the message. He was in total disbelief. Mom and Candis entered the room. Dad let Candis here the message. Her silly butt just started jumping around like a Tigger doll on crack.

"What's all this excitement?" Mom asked with an inquisitive intonation.

Dad handed the phone to Mom and said, "Honey, check this message out that OUR son got today."

Mom's face lit up as she listened. She reached out to grab me for the biggest hug ever. She immediately started making calls to every number she had in her memory bank. Word got out to so many people that our phone started ringing off the hook. Those who didn't call came over to the house. Before you knew it, the Chaney's had a family reunion. The music was cranking and the drinks were flowing. Everyone was excited and happy for me.

"Boy, do you know that your whole life is about to change?" continued to spew from the lips of family and friends. My whole life was about to change. That was something to digest for real. The notoriety, the money, the chicks---all that was getting ready to increase. However, a week later, it was nothing but lights, camera, action, cut and that's a wrap for the day. I was shooting long hour's everyday. By the second episode, I had lines. It wasn't as hard as I thought to memorize them. I got comfortable real quick. I was born for this type of business. Instead of it being a job it became more and more of my life.

As we continued to shoot and the buzz got out about the show, I was doing interviews with other cast members on BET, MTV and all the other popular entertainment networks. I was definitely in a different world at that time.

By the third episode, I had so much dialogue I thought the executives were trying to test me out. I had to deliver, and sure enough, I never missed a beat. Around the fourth episode, I was eligible for something called Screen Actors Guild, (SAG). SAG is the nation's premier labor union representing actors. SAG represents nearly 120,000 actors in film, television, commercials and music videos.

The buzz was spreading about the first season of *The Wire*. This motivated the cast to knock out episodes as the months flew by. I had no time to chill with friends. By the time I got off the set I would be so tired I crashed once I arrived home from Baltimore. The two hour round trip from Forestville, MD to Baltimore, MD was a stretch after working long hours. I was literally pounding the pavement day and night. The moments I wasn't on the set, I was at Melwood. Little did I know the industry parties I looked forward to were the ones I created in my head. They were called, *GET SOME SLEEP*. Hey, it was the cost of show business and I was willing to pay for it. "AND SCENE!"

A MOTHER'S NOTE: SET MY BABY FREE
by Elaine Chaney

When Tray got the role for *The Wire*, Skip and I were very excited. We also felt a little scared because of the character he would portray. As Jehovah's Witnesses we always want what's best for our children. When Tray told us about the cursing, drugs and killing that his character would be doing on the show, our mouths dropped.

"Tray, your mom and I need to talk to the elders at The Hall about this," I remember Skip saying. He was concerned about the elder's reaction to Tray playing a bad guy on television. We needed to let them know our son is now an actor and playing a hard core role on the show. We knew that this would not be a good look as servants of Jehovah. I knew people in the truth would look at our family differently. They knew Tray to be a good kid who would never let a bad word come out of his mouth, kill anyone or become a drug dealer. So his portrayal of a "thug" was a shock to them.

One elder told us that he watched the show, and he could not believe the language that come out of Tray's mouth. There was no other choice but to reprove Tray. Privileges that were once afforded to Tray were now taken away.

Tray use to carry the microphone to the brothers and sisters at The Kingdom Hall when they gave comments on our *Watchtower* literature. Tray also use to give public talks to the congregation. When he was cast for Poot on *The Wire* he was stripped of his religious duties 'cause his role was immoral. This was his second reproof.

While on restriction, a Jehovah's Witness is to recover from spiritual weakness and to impress upon him the importance of respecting God's holiness. So, a person who is spiritually weak may be relieved of certain responsibilities in the congregation of Jehovah's Witnesses until there is evidence of his regaining spiritual strength.

We are all sad that Tray is still on reproof. He is an actor, and we all pray that he can get a more moral role. We want everyone to be able to watch Tray on TV or in theaters without him bringing reproach on Jehovah's name. We are still proud of him. We love him very much, and we know he loves Jehovah.

SEASON TWO EPISODE THREE
Hot & Heavy

I took a big gulp of something I couldn't pronounce or taste 'cause it just burned going down. I looked around with bugged eyes as if she was talking to someone else, but she was talking to me.

"What about your son?" I asked while recovering from the sting of the liquor. I was trying to stall 'cause I was really nervous. I had never spent the night with a woman before. My parents were always quick to let me know that only married couples should sleep together. *If you ain't married, you have no business having sex, kissing, touchin' or nuthin. Ya hear me?* I remember Mom's warning clearly.

"He's gone for the weekend. Don't worry 'bout him. Be more concerned with what I'm gonna to do with you." Kesha didn't blink at all.

I'm thinkin' *Stop playin'! Is this chic for real?* Kesha was no joke. I'm no punk. My Popeye's dreams could come true. I could get breast, legs, and thighs in just a matter of time. I couldn't wait to tap that buttermilk biscuit of hers. Hey, she was serving and I was dining.

I jumped up from the couch and called Mom and Dad to let them know a brother wasn't coming home that night. I had to think of a good lie real quick. I know. Lies are bad, but I'm saying. What would you do in my situation? I was a twenty year-old with raging hormones. I heard, somewhere that if you don't let go of your soldiers you could die. Right? Well, that was my excuse.

I excused myself 'cause I didn't want Kesha to hear me checking in with my parents. They were strict and far from stupid. If I was going to stay out all night, I had better been on the set working late.

Ring! Ring! Fumble! Fumble! Fumble! Mom picks up.

"Tray?"

"Hey Ma!"

"How is the shooting goin'?" she asked instantly.

"It's goin' good so far. That's what I called about. We aren't finished and have to keep shooting all night. The execs are putting us up in hotel tonight. So I'll be home tomorrow." My acting skills were on play.

"Baby that's good that they look out for you that way.

Call me in the mornin'. Be careful and I love you."

"Love you too! Don't forget to tell Dad."

"I won't, honey. Have fun."

I heard Mom talking to Dad before we hung up. I felt bad 'cause my parents didn't deserve my lies. I made up for it later. My hormones were getting in the way of me telling them the truth.

When I got back in the house Kesha was no where to be found. Then out of the blue I heard my name being sung.

"Traaaaay! Come up stairs."

I followed the directions. To my surprise, she was standing in a seductive pose. Kesha was butt naked!

At that moment, I was like *WHOA!* Kesha rushed me, grabbed me by the face and started kissing me *all over my baaaah-dee.* I was usually the one attacking. I guess when a woman knows what she wants, it's no hold bar.

I was in a race against time 'cause the next thing I knew Kesha ripped my shirt off, laid me on the bed and started grabbing for my belt. In less than 10 seconds, my pants were down for the count. She was an alley cat! Baby girl had skills. Kesha was performing sexual acts that made me feel like I was ten feet tall. I couldn't let her get the best of me.

I flipped her over and showed her that I could match her energy. I don't know if it was the liquor or the mere fact that I had the best of this thirty-two year old woman, but I went to work.

When it was finally over, we were both exhausted. In no time flat, she was sleep. Me? I could only lay there thinking to myself, *what the heck did I just do?* My conscience started eating me up. I didn't use a rubber. I was scared to death 'cause I didn't think before making such a drastic move. The after thoughts of casual sex are no fun. My parents warned me that all types of women would be throwing themselves on me after they saw me on TV. They encouraged me to be careful and never allow anyone to trick me. The bad part about that whole situation is that I hadn't been on TV yet and Kesha was one of my cast members.

The next morning, I woke up around 7. Kesha was still sleeping. I woke her up and told her that I had to head back home.

"Kesha, I have to run back to PG." I really didn't have to go anywhere but I told her that 'cause I wanted to get out of her house.

"I know you're not just going to hit and run?" Kesha put it out there.

"Naw baby, I have to go to work. I do have a nine to five job."

"When am I going to see you again?" She ran her finger tips along my exposed arms.

Funny thing is, she was trying to turn me on again, but at that very moment any feelings that I had for her had left me. I got what I wanted from her and I was done. It was time to bounce.

"As soon as I have another shoot, we'll get up again."

I knew it would be another three or four weeks before I was on the set. I wasn't telling Kesha that, 'cause I didn't know how she would react.

"Well, that's fine. I had a really nice time, Tray. I could really see us being a couple."

I don't know what radio station Kesha was listening to, but in my mind, I knew that I didn't want to be with her---mainly 'cause she had baggage. She had a son that was not mine and the second reason was 'cause I didn't want anyone thirty-two years old. She was too old for me. I wanted someone my age or one year older not twelve years older. I'd later eat these words. However, at that time, it was really time for me to go then.

I fed into whatever she was saying to make her feel good, then I gave her a kiss on the cheek and left. On the way home I called my best friend, Eric, my brother from another mother, Zeek and my cousin, Chicago. We were on a four-way phone conversation. The fellaz had to know the dirt I'd gotten myself into. I told them every detail about Kesha. It was laugh fest all the way home. They were cracking up at me.

"Yo, does she have any friends?" Eric asked. Each of them said they want to get in the acting business just so they could sex with as many chicks possible. We were so immature.

The closer I got to my house, I had to keep a straight face and act as if I was on the set all night. I then noticed a funny odor. I sniffed around the car. It was me! I smelled like sex. I had to really creep in the house and jump straight in the shower. I took a detour to try and air out. Boy was I nervous!

Once I reached the house, I noticed that not only were Mom and Dad's cars parked in the driveway, but also my grandparent's van too. *Are you serious,* I sighed to myself. The universe came back to bite you in the butt. Everyone was probably in the kitchen having breakfast. I had to face all of them with hugs and kisses as that was the customary greeting in our family. The moment of truth was near.

I walked up to the door and unlocked it, walked in the house and BAM! Everyone was right in the kitchen like I thought. The machine gun greetings and questions came at me.

"Is that my baby!" Grandma started shouting.

"Hey, Big Time," Granddad greeted me from the dining table. He always referred to his grandchildren by this name.

"How did the shoot go?" Dad asked with wide eyes of excitement.

My game face was on. "It went real good. I'm tired is all. I'm glad they put me in a hotel last night."

Then out of nowhere, Dad gets this frown on his face.

He started walking up to me. I just knew he could smell the Tray and Kesha juice on me. All I could think about was how stupid I was 'cause I didn't take a shower before I left Baltimore.

I stood as far as I could from Dad, but he seemed to move closer and closer to me.

"Tray, what is that smell?" he asked in a very aggressive tone. My heart dropped on the floor. I looked at Grandma and Grandpa as if I didn't have a clue.

"Tray, you been drinkin'? You're reeking liquor."

It got real quiet in the Chaney house. The crickets chirped. All eyes were on me. I swear I saw a pigeon and a squirrel eaves dropping in the bay window.

Action! Again with the lies, I reply, "The cast went to an all night drinking party and I had a few drinks. I'm good. We had a great time."

My parents and grandparents knew that I drank, so they were not mad about that. The activity in the house continued. They all just laughed at me and said they were glad that I stayed in a hotel instead of drinking and drive. I laughed along with them. If only they knew what I was driving the night before, I'd be half-way down the street running from Mom and Dad's belt.

I *could have killed Tray. I remember that whole Kesha incident like it was yesterday. Skip still doesn't know about. I guess he's gonna know now."*

-Elaine Chaney

Kesha blew up the house phone for the entire three to four week period I was off the set. She would call and talk about nothing.

"When we gonna make love again? When you coming up to B-more again? Whatchu doing?"

I was chillin'. When it was time to shoot episodes for *The Wire* again, I didn't call Kesha, 'cause I didn't want to be bothered. I concentrated on all things *The Wire*. After we finished knocking out some re-shoots, the producers told me that I was not needed for the tenth episode so the next time I would come back was for the last three episodes which were eleven, twelve and thirteen. So, I was able to have more chill time with friends and family.

It had been a couple of weeks when I got the craziest phone call of my life.

"Tray, I'm pregnant," Kesha said nonchalantly. I had a suspicion she'd play the *I'm pregnant* card after she talked a whole lot about the bills she couldn't pay.

"My car is about to be repossessed and I might loose my townhouse if I don't come up with the money," Kesha kept complaining. I felt the set up coming.

The moment she called to tell me she needed $400.00 to have an abortion, I knew she was lying. Her voice had no emotion in it. I could not believe what I was hearing from her. My family doesn't believe in abortions. I wasn't getting played. So, I shouted back to her.

"Stop lying! You ain't getting' nuthin from me! If you really pregnant, have the baby and I'll take care of it. You ain't killin' my child!"

Kesha wasn't down with that idea. If I was going to take the burden of taking care of the child, the problem should have been solved. We argued back and forth calling each other every name in the book. Then she pulled the ghetto girl threats out of her hat.

"I'm gonna get my cousin Moe Moe and 'nem to beat you up.?"

Come on! Is she thirty-two or two? She made some more harsh threats, but I didn't really pay them any attention. I knew deep down inside she didn't want people to know about this. Secondly, she didn't know where I lived. She was trying to break me down to give her the money. I don't ordinarily disrespect females, but this was a special circumstance.

As she kept blabbing I got frustrated and hung the phone up. Like a crazy woman, Kesha kept calling back and I kept hanging up. Finally, she didn't call me anymore that day. I didn't hear from her for a week.

One Sunday evening after coming home from the Kingdom Hall, I walked in the kitchen and noticed my mother had just hung the phone up. Mom had this weird look on her face. I tried to go up to her and start playing around. She wasn't feeling me. She didn't even laugh when I tickled her.

"What's going on, Ma?" I asked.

"Tray, who is Kesha?"

With hands on her hip and both her eyebrows shaking hands, Mom was not looking for any run around Robin Hood's barn answers. My mouth dropped.

Before I could think of what to say, she waved a piece of paper in her hand. Kesha's name and number was on it.

"I just got off the phone with this woman and she told me everything. So don't stand up here and lie to me. Tell me the truth." I couldn't believe Kesha called my mother on me. This was getting more and more unreal.

I could see the hurt in Mom's eyes. I fessed up.

I told Mom exactly what went on with me and Kesha. I also told Mom that I didn't believe that Kesha was pregnant, and if she was then she shouldn't be against me taking on the responsibility. I didn't want her to kill the baby.

"Tray, the girl has medical issues that might cause her to die if she goes full term with a pregnancy. So she has to get an abortion."

Mom slammed the paper on the table and started walking around the kitchen. She continued talking, but more to herself trying to figure things out.

"I don't know why she got caught up in such a careless act...old as she is. All these diseases goin' on 'round here and she's playin' 'round with her life. You just don't go 'round having sex with strange men---especially some lil boy almost 10 years younga than you---and for what? To get money? Stupid, I tell you. Just plain stupid!"

Mom hit the kitchen table with her fist. She was hysterical. I backed up 'cause I didn't want to feel her fire.

Then turned to me.

"Now Tray, I told her she's irresponsible and I don't want her calling here no more---" Whew! I was glad about that. "But," Mom paused for a minute to wipe her hands on her apron and then put them on her forehead. "Tray, I'm going to tell you this. You're giving her the money." Her firm index finger pointed directly at me. There was no mistaking who she was talking to. I was shocked she still wanted me to give Kesha the money!

I wined like a baby, "But Maaaa, she's lying! Before all this stuff went down she was telling me how she needed money for her car and her house and---"

"I don't care if she has to get money to pay the Pope, Tray! You don't need this in your life right now. Take money outta your check and pay that girl! And another thing, since when did we teach you to lie about your age?"

I was dumbfounded. I told the truth about that. "Ma, see there she goes lying again. I told her I was twenty."

"Well, looks like to me you two need to be together.

You're both a bunch of liars." I felt smaller than a smurf.

Mom called me out. "The way I see it, both of you will learn a lesson from this. You'll think twice before you test your manhood inside some girl and she will stop playing with fire 'cause she's hot and bothered.

I had to pay the piper 'cause I didn't know any of Kesha's friends or family to verify if she was pregnant or not. Ironically, I was supposed to get a $400.00 check from Melwood that day. That was the only money I would have until my check came in from *The* Wire. I gave the money to Mom to wire to Kesha.

Mom talked to me for three hours that day and I felt so bad about my conduct and about lying to her and Dad. Dad still didn't know about this incident. I asked Mom to promise me that she would not tell him. I knew Dad would go off and I would not have a chance to say a word. We had already been in this situation before and I was already on reprove for taking an immoral role on *The Wire*. I never got a whoopin' up to that point, but somehow I believe that would have been the day I got my first taste of somebody's belt.

Mom talked to me for another three hours about the consequences of my actions. I just prayed I didn't contract any STDs or A.I.D.S. In the grand scheme of things whether Kesha was telling the truth or not, $400 was a small price to pay for my indiscretions. Being careless could have cost lives.

SEASON TWO EPISODE FIVE
My Face on the Tube

After everything was over with the Kesha incident, it was time to get back to business. We had about three more episodes left to shoot for *The Wire*. We got the word from HBO that it would be premiering in June 2002. That meant all I had was a couple more months to wait to see myself on T.V. I couldn't wait!

The last three episodes were amazing for me. In episode, eleven there were scenes where I really stood out. I had to set my best friend up and kill him. One of the execs, David Simon, told me that I would have to shed some tears on this part of the show. I had never just made myself cry before. I was worried that I wouldn't be able to pull it off.

I practiced and practiced crying at home. I didn't have a point of reference to make myself cry. I had this notion that in order to be a good actor, you had to master the art of crying on demand.

It was time to get in front of the producers and directors and play the crying game---minus the shock ending. I started sweating and praying at the same time. I walked up the stairs of the apartment building where the murder was to take place. I stood in front of the camera with the gun in my hand and pointed at my best friend. The tears started to form in my eyes. Drip! I couldn't believe! I did it---cried on demand. Two points for Tray! Swish! The executives were impressed. I was a hit!

We wrapped up the first season, and my character didn't die. Now it was time for vacation. The production office took some time off to get the second season together. The cast members and I were invited to a wrap party and they gave us shirts, hats, jackets and other items branded with *The Wire* logo on it.

A number of us used the time off to shop resumes and headshots for additional work. The months went by so fast that I almost forgot that I had to get back to reality. Melwood was still my employer as well.

I'm glad I had something to keep me occupied while waiting for the show to air. I couldn't wait to hear feedback about my performance. June was only two weeks away, but the anticipation was crazy. The promotion efforts for *The Wire* were heavy. People were calling me saying they saw me on previews and the radio stations were talking about me. The producers told me that it would be like this once they started to promote the show.

When Sunday finally arrived, Mom and Dad planned a huge premier party at the house. It was the usual Chaney throw down, and I was the guest of honor.

Mom and Aunt Peedie were in the kitchen cooking up a storm. They whipped up Teriyaki chicken, barbecue meatballs, tuna macaroni salad, green bean and desserts out the ying yang. Of course there were plenty of drinks from Kool-Aid to alcohol. It was a celebration.

The music was jumping and everyone was partying. It felt so good to see the happy faces of my family and friends. Mom was so excited that she made sure everyone knew her baby was going to be on television. She even made flyers with my pictures on them so people wouldn't forget to watch the show's premier.

Ten o'clock! It was time for the show to come on. Flash! There I was---all over the television. You would think we were watching the Super Bowl 'cause every time I appeared, there were cheers and screams of excitement. All I could do was laugh. They would scream so loud that I couldn't hear what the character after me said next. It was cool though, 'cause I was recording it and could see the show later. This was not just my time. This was a moment my entire family could live.

As soon as everyone left I played the show back. As much as I loved my family and friends, I promised myself that I wouldn't watch the rest of the episodes with them 'cause I really wanted to enjoy the content to perfect my performances for the next season. Even in the midst of me watching the show, the telephone started to ring off the hook. People called to tell me how much they enjoyed seeing me on TV. They wished, however, I had some speaking parts. I had to explain to them that I didn't have a speaking role on the first show 'cause it was just the pilot. They would have to be cool until the next episode.

"Your life is about to change," a friend shouted in my ear after seeing me appear on the premier of *The Wire.*

That was the second time I heard those words. The next day, I saw the change manifest itself in my new world.

SEASON TWO EPISODE SIX
Drive Time. Dinner Time.

I was on I495 in Maryland headed to Melwood. A car drove close to me. When I turned to look, it was a car full of girls screaming and waving their hands. I had never seen them before so I turned away and kept driving. They continued to beep the horn and yelled something at me. I was curious and decided to roll down my window to check 'em out.

"Scuse me, ain't you that guy from *The Wire*? I saw you last night on the show beating up that white boy"?

I just shook my head yes and they went ballistic! I sped up and laughed. I couldn't believe that people watched television that hard, 'cause again, I didn't say a word. On the strength of me showing up in some scenes I was recognized. I thought to myself, *Man, what are they going to do once I have speaking parts.*

Each day after that more and more people started recognizing me. It was unreal. I told Mom and Dad about it and they looked at me like they didn't believe me. Then one day when the family went Red Lobster, they saw the truth.

As we ate, a group of girls at the next table kept looking over at us and whispered among themselves. I didn't pay them much attention until Candis spoke up and said, "Look ya'll, they're talkin' 'bout Tray."

"See, I told ya'll how people act when they see me!" I had proof now.

One of the girls came over to the table.

"Excuse me, I apologize for starring at you...but are you that guy from *The Wire*?"

I said, "Yes." It wasn't too long before I was grabbed and kissed by random women. This young lady asked me to come over to her table and meet some of her girlfriends. I went and all five of them asked me questions about the show. I put on my mack mode.

"Ladies, I can't discuss the details of the show. You'll just have to keep watching the show on Sundays," I said as cool as I could. I might have been an amateur, but I couldn't let them know it.

They all wanted my autograph. This was something I wasn't use to doing either. Quiet dinners with my family were definitely out now. It was wild, but I loved that attention. I felt just like a movie star.

By the time I got back to my family, my food was ice cold. Everybody else had finished eating. Dad paid the bill. We tried to leave the restaurant, but people kept stopping me before I got to the door.

"We like your work on the show, keep it up!" encouraging fans continued to give me accolades. Even some of the employees at Red Lobster came from the kitchen to talk to me. A few of them had cameras and wanted to take pictures before I left. It was all good. I was getting what I asked for.

I loved the fact that I actually started to have a fan base. Knowing the attention would increase once HBO aired the episodes with my speaking roles, I invested in a fine point Sharpie.

With so much attention flowing my way, I decided to use my new celebrity status to my advantage. It was time to hit the night clubs.

I tried to get in some of the hot spots in the D.C. area. I still had not turned twenty-one, but I was going to push the envelope to see if I could at least get passed the door.

The fellaz and I got together and headed to Dream, as it was called then.

"Eye Dee," the bouncer commanded.

I immediately stepped back and Chicago, my big mouth cousin, was so proud of me being on TV that he had to let the unknowing brutha know it.

"Do you know who this is, man? This is Poot from HBO's *The Wire!*" Chicago shouted loud enough for aliens to hear.

"Chill, man. Don't do that out here," I spoke to Chicago trying to seem modest while looking around to see who else heard him.

I wanted people to recognize me on their own. If they didn't know who I was at that time, I surely wasn't going to go through that whole routine of explaining my part in the show. However, this dude at the door whose badge said *TAZ* was just not buying it. I didn't want any trouble. I tried to show some of my acting skills by lying. I told Taz that I was 21 years old but left my ID at home.

"I don't care who you are! You ain't gettin' in without an ID!" TAZ said with folded arms lookin' swole.

I was embarrassed 'cause people passed me going into the club and whispered, "That's the lil dude from *The Wire.*" I had a stupid look on my face 'cause being on TV wasn't enough to slip by TAZ.

Darell, Chicago, Zeek and my Uncle Mark were not really pressed to go inside the club anyway. We just cut our losses and rolled out to look for somewhere else to go.

No sooner than we hooked an about face, I heard a voice calling me.

"Hey dude from *The Wire?* How many people you got with you?" some strange dude asked.

Chicago tapped me on the shoulder and pointed in the direction of the voice. When I looked around, it was this short, half bald, middle-aged white guy.

I went up to him with a little apprehension. He started smiling.

"Why? What's the problem?" I asked.

He extended his hand to greet me. "Mike Esterman. I'm the official celebrity agent for D.C.," he stated.

I reached out to shake his hand with one eyebrow raised.

"Say, I watched you go through all that hassle. Come on! You're my guest tonight," Mike insisted.

I looked at the fellaz. They gave me the okay nod and we jumped in line with Mike. He later jumped to the front of the line and whispered something to Taz. It was nothing but bright lights in the city from that point on.

"My apologies, sir. Enjoy your time at Dream," Taz said.

When we first stepped on the scene, we were bammas who couldn't get in. Now, my crew flossed VIP wrist bands. It was on now. I was like, *Whoever this Mike Esterman dude is, his pull is strong!* People all around gave Mike pounds like he was Mr. Hollywood or something. That's what's up.

The music was popping and so were the ladies with their weaves swingin' in the air and bodies bouncing right along to the beat. The fellaz seemed to have poured bottles of cologne on themselves. I guess they hoped to draw the attention of a cute girl or something. The bar was full and the wall flowers were making sure the drywall wasn't coming down.

Mike was on his job. He introduced me to everyone he could find. He pointed and said, "This kid, right here, is a huge actor, he plays "Poot" on HBO's *The Wire!*" Mike yelled over the music. He was pumpin' me up. I wasn't gonna stop him either.

Mike was buying Moet like it was going out of style. The women noticed and swarmed us like we were NBA stars. They were beautiful women puttin' top models to shame. I was sucked into the limelight, and my cousins and uncle were sucked in right along with me. It was off the chain. Word got out that "Tray was in the building," but the party was just beginning.

"Are you enjoying yourself?" Mike asked.

"Shoot! Man, I'm having a ball," I replied.

"Good! Let's go to another floor."

"It's whatever, man!"

I motioned for the fellaz to follow us up the stairs. We entered *The Penthouse*. The atmosphere was indeed different from the rest of the club. I assumed this was exclusive to VIP guests.

Mike showed me around and introduced me to different people that he knew. When I turned toward the door, I couldn't believe who was stepping through the threshold of the VIP.

"Man it can't be! This is unbelievable!" Chicago shouted. Through the crowds of people, we got a glimpse of Mr. Murder Inc. himself. It was JaRule. Here I was a reject at the door at first who was now on the brink of rubbing elbows with one the hottest dudes in hip hop. Mike brought me out of my daze and grabbed me by the arm.

"C'mon. We're going over to kick it with JaRule."

"Straight," I replied with no complaints.

I got my pimp walk on---you know real cool like I belonged. "Hey Ja, this is…."

"Tray Chaney, man!" I gave JaRule a pound.

"Yeah…uh…he plays Poot on…." He starts snapping his fingers to remember. *"The Wire, right?"*

"Yeah!" I said in surprise.

"Yeah, man I'm a fan. I love the show! It's a good hood kind of show." JaRule was giving the show its just do and remembered my character. I was impressed.

We gave each other more dap and continued to party like we'd been hitting the clubs together on a regular. What a night.

The night had started to die down and we were all lit from drinking the "bubbly." I drank so much of it until I had the worse case of hick-ups that I had ever had in my life. I became the butt of jokes as we walked out the door.

In between our laughter, Mike gave me his business card.

"Call me in the morning so we can discuss your future. We can get you booked at some of the other clubs in the city---make you some money. Ya know?" Mike advised.

Make some money doing what? That was the first question I had in my head. I couldn't image people paying me to host a club in D.C. This wasn't such a bad idea. I could more than recoup that $400 from my Kesha moment.

"Thanks, Mike. I appreciate everything you did for us tonight. I'll call you in the morning." I stuffed Mike's card tightly in my pocket.

On the way home, Chicago and I compared notes on all the girls we booked that night. Chicago had racked up at least twenty phone numbers, and I matched his twenty give or take a few.

"Man, what's it gonna be like when we have millions of dollars." Chicago was exaggerated in his movements. He scraped imaginary money close to his body.

"Bananas!" I replied.

Blingaling! My cell rang. It was Darell and Uncle Mark. They were driving in front of us. Uncle Mark suggested we grab something to eat. You know where we were headed. In LA, the spot is Roscoe's Chicken and Waffles. On the east coast, IHOP was the late night restaurant of choice. That was a bet. I was hungry anyway from all the excitement.

The phone rang again. It was Mom.

"Tray where are you? It's 4 in the morning. I woke up worried 'bout you."

"Mom, you're not going to believe the night we had. We're 'bout to grab something to eat then I'll be home. I promise!"

I comforted Mom. She was assured I'd be safe and hung up the phone.

It was after 6 when I arrived home. As soon as I opened the door, Dad was standing at the top of the stairs.

"Who is that coming in my house at this time of morning?" Wiping his eyes and yawning, Dad knew it was me.

"It's me Dad. Sorry for coming in like this, but I had a wild and crazy night."

"Oh, you think you grown, Mr. TV Man? Tell me about this wild night." Dad headed down the stairs while I made myself comfortable on the couch.

I broke it down for him from our run in with *TAZ* down to all the numbers we gathered from the ladies. I had to explain who JaRule was, but that was fine. He got real excited about my network connection through Mike Esterman.

"You want me to set your alarm so you can call him in the morning?" Dad offered.

"Naw, Dad. I got this. Trust me. I won't forget." I responded.

"Well, look…I'm glad you're home in one piece. I'm going back to sleep. But next time, you're taking me with you. You ain't the only one 'round here supposed to be having fun." Dad spun around like he was a member of the Temptations.

"Alright Dad, you got it! But you can't be bussin' moves like that. The ladies will run from us." I laughed gave him a pound before he headed up the stairs.

I posted up on the sofa in the basement. As fast as I fell asleep, I should have won a medal of speed sleeping. I was still a bit anxious about calling Mike, though.

I woke up from my 2 hour nap with the anticipation, cleared my sleepy throat and dialed Mike's number. The voicemail came on. I left a message to make sure he knew I followed through. An hour later, the phone rang. It was Mike.

"How do you think things went last night?" Mike asked.

"It was cool. I really enjoyed myself," I responded.

"Well in my eyes, everything wasn't cool!" he said.

Mike felt I should be getting paid for making public appearances, and he didn't understand why this was not happening. He was even concerned about me having problems getting into clubs, especially in the Washington, D.C. since I was from the area. I was becoming a local celebrity.

"Do you have anyone representing you?"

"Yes. As a matter of fact I have Linda Townsend Management as my representative." I was proud to report this information.

"Hmph," was all I heard. Mike kind of gave me the impression that Linda was not the best person to speak on my behalf.

"Look, Tray, people will come to the clubs to see celebrities and pay good money each and every week."

"For real?" My eyebrows started doing a little dance.

"That's where you come in, Tray. You need to start working with me and I can get you paid gigs."

Mike was the first person who ever told me something like this. So I was really interested 'cause extra money was something that I really needed. I had to let this dude meet Mom and Dad and tell them the same thing he just told me. I wasn't trying to get caught up in any scams. I was new to the business which meant people were going to try and take advantage of me. My character may not have been the sharpest knife in the drawer on television with nothing but women on the mind, but the real Tray Chaney wasn't playing with his ends.

"This sounds good, Mike. But we're gonna have to set up some time to speak specifics."

Hmm. I sure felt like I was becoming more mature despite the youthful look I gave on and off the screen. It was my face and my money. No one was coming between the two of them. So everything had to be legit.

COMMERCIAL BREAK
I'm a Video Guy

The Wire was going great; I traveled all over, getting $2,000.00 to appear and host parties around the country, thanks to my dude Mike Esterman. He's still down with me for life. Linda Townsend Management called with another opportunity.

"Tray, a couple of directors called the office today and said they want you to be in a video," she says.

"Cool, do I get to dance?" I asked remembering what put me on in the first place. What I wouldn't give to show my moves again.

"No. They want you to play a character named Andre, opposite of a rapper named Bow Wow," Linda replied.

When Linda said Bow Wow, I literally dropped the telephone.

My mouth was wide open with excitement. I couldn't believe what she said.

"Tray? Tray? Are you still there?"

Finally gaining my composure, I was able to speak again. "Yeah! Yeah! I'm here."

"Good. I thought I lost you. As I was saying, you will be playing a character by the name of Andre. Now, let me warn you, he is abusing his girlfriend and Bow Wow is trying to tell her to stay away from you and get with him," Linda explained.

I could have been break dancing naked in front of a bunch of baby rabbits and I would have still accepted the role. Okay, not naked, but the mere fact the opportunity was presented to me was unbelievable. This video was going to be broadcast worldwide. Grant it, I would be seen as a bad guy, but it was another dream come true.

I would be seen on MTV, BET, and VH1. More money more fame---was all I could think about. The directors, Randy Marshall & Eric Williams of The Fat Catz, are major hitters in the music industry. They saw me on *The Wire* and loved my character. I got cast on the strength of that alone.

The video was so hot that it remained number 1 on 106th and Park for weeks. They had to retire that joint 'cause it was in rotation so much. Thanks, Bow Wow and The Fat Catz for giving this little dancing kid from PG a chance.

SEASON THREE EPISODE ONE
When Art Meets Life Part I: Being Down.

I got a call while visiting the production office for *The Wire*. It was my right-hand-man Zeek. He had just come home from jail like a week before the phone call. We kept in touch through letters, but he wanted to know how everything was going since I was on *The Wire*. You know---was I totally different now 'cause I was in the limelight?

As soon as I got off the set, I called Zeek and we linked up. Imperial Park Apartments was where kicked it. The convenient store was on the corner. It was owned by a young, black dude named Rick. He kept it simple and named the store Rick's Mini-Mart. Near Rick was the spot where we got our shape-ups, the neighborhood barbershop Barber One.

We loved hanging around there when time allowed. Man I was happy to see my homeboy Zeek. I hated to hear that he was locked up, but he stayed in behind bars. I never thought he committed any crimes that serious for the police to lock him up. But hey, breaking the law is breaking the law.

Zeek and I were sitting in my car reminiscing about old times when a dude named Kevin walked up. Kev used to go to school with us. We kicked it, talked about *The Wire* and then he eased his way into the neighborhood gossip.

"Man, don't worry about what Black said," Kevin just came out the blue with that statement.

"Man, what are you talkin' 'bout?" Zeek asked.

Black was a tall dark skinned dude who lived around Imperial Park.

"Oh you didn't hear? Chicago and Black got into it 'bout a chick Chicago was trying to holla at! Chicago was out numbered by Black and his crew. So Chicago was going to get back at him that Tuesday night." I couldn't believe bammaz were still fighting over girls.

Kevin kept talking 'bout how Chicago didn't want him to say anything to me or Zeek 'cause if we heard, we'd be on it.

Okay, so here is where things get funny. I'm an actor portraying a wild character on TV and I was living the life in reality. I was leading a double life, one on camera and one off camera. My parents didn't know this side of me. I could get down with the best of them in the streets, but being busy sort of kept me out of the life. As violent as the content is on *The Wire,* it was becoming a life saver.

I couldn't punk out, despite all I would put on the line. Black and his crew were around the corner from us. So Zeek and I started to brainstorm on how we were going to handle things.

My cousin, Boo, pulled up and said, "Tray did you hear what happened between Black and Chicago?" It was on now 'cause everyone knew.

"I was waiting for Chicago to come around here with the rest of the crew so we could get Black," Boo exclaimed.

"Why you need all these people for one fool?" Zeek asked.

I was sitting there thinking the same thing.

"You right! We gone handle this right now!" I sound like I was on the set---right on cue.

We made a stop at Crazy Ed's crib. He was the friend we went to for a very specific reason. We weren't coming to hang out and drink Capri Suns. Crazy Ed kept heat. Whenever we knocked on his door, he knew what was up.

Crazy Ed was a family man with a girlfriend and two little ones. They all lived together. He seldom came outside unless he was on his way to work. Ed was the most unsuspecting dude---despite the full beard, he had an innocent look about him. He looked like the kid you'd invite over for dinner if his mom's locked him out. You felt bad for him, but your family just loved him. Any way, we knocked on the door. Crazy Ed looked out the peephole and saw us. By the time he opened the door, he had on leather gloves and was like, "Alright, where we going?"

Me, Boo, Zeek and Crazy Ed headed to where Black and his crew were chillin'. As we got closer, Boo kept saying how he was going to knock Black out. Some other choice words were used, but I'll reserve that for your imagination.

Black and his crew, sure enough, were rolling dice on the corner. When they saw us, the crap game stopped instantly!

"What cha'll wanna do?" Black asked with both hands out flexin'.

The next thing you know this dude named Big Lou punched Boo in the face out of no where! This was a shock 'cause Big Lou hung with us on occasions. We thought he was our friend. I guess he was doing what he had to do so he wouldn't look bad with his *new crew*. Whatever.

The next thing we saw was Zeek hit Big Lou and they went toe to toe. Boo rushed Black and I started helping Zeek beat on Big Lou until Big Lou fell to the ground. Crazy Ed chilled making sure nothing got outta hand. Then Big Lou lifted his shirt and starts reachin'. This fool pulled out a 44 caliber.

POW! POW! POW! Big Lou started buckin' all over the place.

The gun went off and everyone hit the ground and froze. Crazy Ed reached for his gun. Then Zeek surprisingly pulled out a 9 milometer. I didn't know what was getting ready to go down. I wish there was someone to yell *Cut* or *That's a wrap until tomorrow* or somethin'. No voices from the studio speakers yelled to my aid. This surely wasn't television. I couldn't change the channel 'cause I was in the thick of things now.

After struggling with Big Lou, Zeek got his gun. At that point, we kicked, punched and stomped Big Lou until blood was flying everywhere. Big Lou was sprawled out in a puddle of his own fluids. He was helpless. Zeek made it worse and grabbed Big Lou by his head and stuck the gun in his mouth. He cocked it back. I started sweating, Zeek started yelling.

"Tray, should I pull the trigger? Let me kill this nigga!"

Zeek was begging for confirmation.

Everyone was quiet. I grabbed Zeek by his hand and said, "Man, you just got out," I spoke lightly. "Don't do it."

Zeek finally let Big Lou go. Big Lou walked off and eventually collapsed in the middle of the street. The whole neighborhood looked at us. We were covered with Big Lou's blood. We started to hear sirens and an ambulance. It was time to jet. This was one scene I didn't want to repeat again. It was just way too much going on in one moment. I really needed a commercial break from this episode of my life.

SEASON THREE EPISODE TWO
When Art Meets Life Part II: What Was That?

All was quiet in the neighborhood. The house was still. Everyone was asleep. Dad was usually the first to get up 'cause he had to be at work at 5:30 AM. Normally, he danced to the tune of the alarm clock. There was one particular morning that had all of us ducking and diving. Gunshots were right outside my parent's window.

Bomb! Bomb! Bomb! As soon as Mom heard the shots she instantly jumped on the floor. Dad was right beside her. Aunt Peedie and Candis were crawling down the hall on fours. I slept in the basement so I didn't hear a thing until I heard the sirens from the police cars. They were in front of our house.

"Tray! Someone shot up your car!" Dad ushered me up the steps. My heart was beating so hard that it seemed as if it was 'bout to come through my chest. We peeked through the curtains. PG County's finest were taking notes and wanted names.

"We'd betta go out there and talk to them," Dad said.

Once we got outside, a PG cop asked us if we knew who the car belonged to.

"It's my father's car, but I drive it." I gave an honest answer.

"Son, do you know who might be behind this?" the officer asked.

"Naw...Naw. I don't."

Deep down inside I knew who was been behind this. I didn't think they'd retaliate in this manner.

PGPD wrote up a report and told me to be careful 'cause by the looks of things someone was out to get me.

"This is a warning message for something," the officer said.

All I could do was put my head down 'cause I didn't want to tell anyone what really took place.

The officers drove off and my family went back in the house. At the kitchen table, my peeps didn't know what to make of everything that was going on.

Mom came down the stairs and she instantly gave me this look like she knew I was involved in something.

"Tray, what are you into that we don't know about, son?"

Dad tried to sound as concerned as he could to scrape out the truth. This was his interrogation tactic. So I started talking.

"See what had happened was last week right after I came back from the production office and stuff and I went outside with Boo and Zeek and Boo wanted to play a little basketball so he asked a couple of guys who were on the court to play him one on one and this guy named Black stepped up and challenged Boo and Black got mad all 'cause Boo showed him up on the basketball court and he was so mad and embarrassed that he decided to pick a fight with Boo and once me and Zeek saw him getting' the best of Boo we jumped in the fight and beat up Black and his friend Big Lou too," I said all this in one breath---no commas periods or exclamation points.

Mom and Dad both knew that Boo could play basketball really well. So I made up a good story leading them to believe that this whole situation was over a basketball game. I never wanted my parents, especially Mom, to know there was a gun involved in the actual story. She would have freaked out. Mom didn't like guns. I had to change the story around to make it look like it wasn't nothin' that bad to make these guys come in front of our house and shoot up the car.

I knew exactly who it was that did this horrible thing to my family and the way I knew it was 'cause of what my neighbor Bug told me. He said he was looking out of his window as soon as he heard gun shots and he noticed a white van with two guys with hoods on their heads. One of the guys had a double barrel shot gun in his hand. He deliberately shot at the gas tank. The bamma was trying to blow up the whole block and himself.

Each bullet that hit the car bounced off the side of Bug's house. The bullet holes are still on Bug's property to this day. He said they're reminders of what happened that morning.

By 7:00 AM, my phone was ringing off the hook. I got calls from my cousins Darell, Chicago, Boo and Shawn. They all heard what went down and they were on their way to my house. Once they got there, we started cleaning up the glass.

It was a very sad time for us all. I guess I was the likely target seeing I had the most to loose. Even still, all of us were walking nervously in circles. I could see the headlines now:

The Wire Star Shoots His Own Movie.

Once we got the glass cleaned up, Shawn called all of us together.

"For these niggaz to do something like this, they mean business. We have to watch our backs at all times. So I'll be sittin' right here on Tray's front porch everyday for a few months...just to protect the house," Shawn volunteered.

He became our personal guard. It caused some suspicion in Mom's eyes, though.

"Why is everyone standing in front of our house, Tray?" she asked.

"Ah, Ma, they just chillin," I said to make Mom feel better.

I wish I wasn't trying to be so hard and just walked away from the situation all together. I never wanted anything like this to fall on the heads of my family. I had to find some way to be more careful about the company I kept or at least delete the scenes that would put the life of my family in jeopardy.

Mom had to ride the Metro bus to work in fear each morning. She would come home frantic 'cause she thought every white van on Suitland Road that rolled by carried the bammaz who shot up my car. I was responsible for that fear inside her. That didn't make me feel good.

I was able to convince Dad to buy another car so Mom could drive to work instead of riding the bus. He listened. Mom had a brand new car that following weekend and she has never been on another bus or train since then. I'm sorry I put you guys through this. I really am.

Something had to give with all this violence. Something had to give. Television or reality? I had a choice to make. The odds of me surviving each season of *The Wire* seemed greater than my own life. I'm no script writer, but at the rate I was going, I was killing myself off my own show. I needed some executives in my reality. I wish the details of my life were made up, but unfortunately, this is the truth I couldn't BeTRAY.

COMMERCIAL BREAK
A Trip Down Memory Lane

I t's no secret that my life was headed down the wrong path. I knew it, but so did my parents. They were getting to the point where they didn't know what to do with me!

I was so caught up with women, drinking, drugs and being wild that I was loosing site of my goals an aspirations. One side of me wanted to leave all of the trouble alone and get back into the entertainment world. I didn't care if it was dancing, acting, or rapping on top of the roof. I needed to be more constructive with my time. So I started thinking...you know, about good times---special moments that made me dream big dreams.

Uncle Jimmy once suggested that I take a vacation to get my head together. He thought going out to Los Angeles would do me some good. It was the most obvious choice for someone who loved the limelight.

I had no clue where I was going to stay. We didn't have family out there. However, Uncle Jimmy's invested interest in my safety prompted him to call in a favor to a celebrity friend.

"Tray, it's Uncle Jimmy. Guess who's on the line?"

"Hey, Tray, I'm flying you out to LA to spend some time with me," the mystery voice said.

"Hey, man, thanks for the opportunity. But I'm sorry I'm not sure who this is."

Then out of the blue, Uncle Jimmy's friend started singing one of the hottest wedding songs out, "For You."

"KENNY LATTIMORE!" I shouted in the receiver. "Wassup, Kenny?" I was geeked.

"I'm good. I heard you want to come to LA for a while."

"Yeah man. I need to get away and do something different, and see how the stars live."

"Well you can come to my crib and chill with me," Kenny suggested.

"Man, I would love to do that. Is next Saturday good?"

"Fine with me. I'll send my driver to the airport to pick you up. Let me make some arrangements and I'll call you back and tell you what time your flight leaves. Is that cool?"

"That's better than cool! It's great! I'll be ready," I said with unbelievable excitement. All was a go.

My flight left out of BWI airport. I was up early but didn't mind. I was going to the city where magic was made and dollar bills changed hands. LA is where the stars come out.

When my plane landed, I didn't know what to expect. I grabbed my carry on bag and headed to baggage claim. It was star treatment from that moment on.

A sign reading "Tray Chaney" caught my attention. It was in the hands of a complete stranger wearing shades. I walked in the direction of the stranger with a confident stroll.

"Hi, Tray. I'm Kenny's assistant. We shook hands and I was escorted outside to a shiny, black Mercedes Benz that was off the hook bling!

The front passenger door opened. Kenny jumped out to greet me with the biggest hug as if we were family. The tripped out thing was, in a way we were. My parents grew up with him.

Palm trees lined the streets in Kenny's neighborhood. Luxury and sports cars were my eye candy. It was like a big car dealership for any boy whoever played the "That's my car" game. I was in my own movie of life. The people had a swagger about them that even if they were having a bad day, they looked good on the outside. Even the dogs walked with confidence.

When we arrived to Kenny's house, he showed me to the guest room. "You playin', right?" I asked.

"Naw, man, this is all you," Kenny said.

I thought I was in Kenny's room---it was like a master bedroom. I was all over the bed like it was a pallet of clouds in heaven. Before I knew it, jet lag set in and I went to sleep. I was spread eagle and probably got my snore on something serious.

Around 8PM, Kenny knocked on my bedroom door.

"Tray, you wanna go to the Angie Stone concert?" Kenny asked.

Did I? "Sure, I would love to go," I managed to say with a groggy voice. I had to get ready for my LA experience and put on some new gear. If paparazzi were anywhere near Kenny and me I wanted to be prepared for my debut shot.

We got to the concert hall and fans bum rushed Kenny. "Stay close to me, Tray," Kenny warned. I didn't mind the attention so much. I liked the attention even if it was second hand.

After getting passed the crowds of people waiting to get into see Angie Stone, Kenny took me to meet with Ms. Stone herself. Mom loves her music and I couldn't wait to tell her about it. I tried not to seem overly excited, but something inside me surfaced to the outside. Ms. Stone was cool about it.

Angie Stone hugged me as if she had known me forever. After being formally introduced, I saw this tall, grinning brutha making his way to the room. It was Magic Johnson.

Click! Flash! Click! The cameras were on overload. I was just glad to be on the other side of the lenses with all these celebrities. This was where I wanted to be on a regular basis. It was a good thing I did make that wardrobe change.

Meeting magic was one thing, but Kenny made wonders happen. He took me to a meeting with Steveland Morris. That's right! I met Stevie Wonder.

When I told my parents, I could feel the percussion from their hearts beating.

"BOY! Do you know who Steve Wonder is? He's a legend!"

Dad screamed in the phone. I wish he could have been there with me.

Kenny and I rolled up to the gated community. I was in still in disbelief that I was getting ready to kick it with the man who drops any song and make it a classic.

"Is this Stevie's house?" I asked Kenny.

"No, this is just the place where he works to do his music." WHOA! This joint was huge! I couldn't begin to imagine what his house looked like.

We were buzzed into the gate like regulars. I was cool as if this was the norm for me as well. Once inside the house, we walked in one room and sat down. Stevie walked in with his assistant---smiling. Kenny stood up and hugged Stevie.

"Hey, Kenny man, how ya doin'?"

"Nuthin, much man." It was time for my introduction. "Stevie, this is my friend Tray Chaney. He's visiting me from Maryland for a few days. This young man has big dreams.

"Follow your dreams and don't give up doing what you want to do in life."

What wonderful words to live by. I planned to follow them as sure as the stars were bright. I wanted to be a shining next to them.

SEASON THREE EPISODE THREE
I'm not Muslim, But I Showed Up at *The Mecca*

Sean P. Diddy Combs, as he was called at the time, was holding auditions for *Making of the Band* at Howard University's Cramton Auditorium. WPGC 95.5FM was broadcasting live. That was a signal for me to get myself prepared to show my face. Every opportunity was my opportunity, no matter how great or small.

The casting crew was looking for singers and rappers. You know me...I was still a dancing machine. It always got me in the door whether the auditions called for a dancer or not. My faithful cousin, Chicago, rolled with me to the auditions. Georgia Avenue was as busy as ever. Trying to park on Howard's campus was anything but a treat. We had to park a mile away and then propped ourselves in a line of what seemed to be seven hundred patient stars in the making. I made seven hundred one.

Whenever our number was called, it was worth it.

While we scooted along, one of the workers from PGC, who passed out forms noticed me.

"Hey! What are you doing?" he blurted out in my direction. I didn't know him from Adam.

Chicago became my unofficial bodyguard. "What you mean?" Chicago asked looking him up and down as if the guy had crossed a line or something.

"My bad, man. I'm Shack-n-da-Pack. I love *The Wire*! You're a star! You don't need to be in the back of the line like this."

We shook hands. "I'm Tray, man."

"Man, follow me," he said.

Chicago and I looked at each other in confirmation. We weren't going to pass up the chance to move to the front of the line.

As we walked by all the people still in line, we noticed everyone was looking and whispering. A series of *I told you that was him!* began to circulate down the line.

I was later introduced to Reggie Rouse, a PGC producer. He also complimented me on my role on the show and immediately advanced me to be the next to perform.

The casting director pumped *Hypnotized* by the Nortorious B.I.G. and I was like a wind up toy---handstands and all. Everyone was amazed. I had my 60 seconds of fame with Puffy's camp. The mere fact that they saw me was enough, and I walked off the stage as if I owned it. That's when I bumped into Freaky-Ty.

Freaky-Ty and I used to kick it back when I was in local talent shows. He used to host the joints. Now we both had big names behind us. Freaky-Ty of WPGC and Tray Chaney of HBO.

"Man, we have to get you live on the air with my girl, Michel Wright!" Freaky-Ty suggested.

My nerves started to dance harder than I did on Cramton's stage. I had always been a fan of Michel's, but I never expected to be one of the people she interviewed---live no less.

Ty escorted Chicago and me to the PGC tour bus. BAM! There she was, Ms. Michel Wright---looking just as beautiful as she sounds on the radio. Her skin was golden brown. Her shape was gorgeous. She was all woman. Get it ma!

Michel was in the middle of a commercial break and I was introduced soon after.

"Ms. Wright---"

"Please call me Michel." She extended her hand.

"Michel, my family and I love your show."

"Aw, thank you."

We chatted for a moment and exchanged numbers. Before I knew it, Michel was given the count down.

"Five. Four. Three. Two." We were live.

"Wassup, people all over the world? This is your girl Michel Wright and next to me I have my little brother chillin' with me. He's on one of the hottest TV shows on the planet.

Introduce yourself to the audience."

"Wassup, world? I'm Tray Chaney from the HBO series *The Wire* and I'm out here with my sister Michel Wright supporting this Diddy joint." That wasn't too bad.

We did a brief interview about my character on the show and toward the end of the program she told me to wish one of the radio personalities a Happy Birthday. That did it. I was responsible for the dead air. I froze up. Thank God Michel was a professional.

"Yeah people, the cat got Tray's tongue! We love you just the same Tray Chaney. He's DC's own. Watch *The Wire* every Sunday at 9PM."

When we were off the air, I had to explain my sudden silence.

"Michel, I'm sorry for freezing up live on the radio, but my religion does not allow me to wish people a Happy Birthday," I explained.

"Oh! What religion do you practice?" Michel asked.

"Jehovah's Witness," I replied.

"Tray, I respect you as a man. I love the way you stand up for what you believe. Call me next week. I want you to appear on my local cable show.

"That's a bet, sis!"

After Michel found out I loved to dance, she asked me to show the rest of her audience that I was more than an actor. I actually had other talents.

The entire family prepped me for my one on one with Michel Wright. Uncle Jimmy showed me how to dress, sit, walk and talk. Mom and Dad coached me through my routine. I had two minutes to get my boogie on and I was determined not to miss a beat.

When I arrived at the studio, Michel hugged me like family. I was then introduced to the other guests she had on the show: a local boxed named Darell Coley and a husband and wife singing duo, Kindred. I would be the first to go on.

After Michel's sound check, it was time to shine.

Michel introduced me as if I was Denzel Washington or something. It was wild. The crowd went crazy when I walked out.

"I love you, Tray," someone yelled from the audience.

In my best celebrity voice, I replied, "I love you too."

We cut the fool for a few and then Michel showed a clip from the show. We then we segued into my surprise performance.

"Tray, we've seen you on *The Wire*. You have the acting thing down. What my audience in the studio and in TV Land don't know is that you can also dance. Can you show us your moves?"

"Michel, baby, I have something way more than just a move, I have a whole routine prepared for you!

The beat dropped for Usher "*You Don't Have to Call*". I had my Dob hat, leather Michael Jackson jacket on and a cane. I know the jacket may have been a little dated, but the crowd still went nuts. They rocked right along with me.

And when I did a split, it was over!

"Go Tray! Go Tray!" came from the audience as if I was back at the Apollo.

When I was done, Michel gave me a hug and a kiss on the Cheek.

"Tray, you're a star in the sky. You were born to entertain. I love you, little brother," Michel said with joy.

Since our first encounter, we stayed in touch. I occasionally get major shout outs on the radio from her. Before my final bow out of the studio, Darryl Coley's publicist introduced herself.

"Hi Tray. I'm Natasha."

SEASON THREE EPISODE FOUR
The Nortorious N.A.T.

She stood about 5 feet or less. Her skin was a beautiful, dark Hersey's chocolate. Hair---as long as Pocohontas. Real or not, she was wearing it well. Her physical appearance was striking, to say the least. This curvy, short, and alluring woman was dressed in a business suit. I noticed her noticing me. Without fail, she made her presence known.

"I'm Natasha Rennie, your future publicist." Out of this beauty's mouth came the voice of confident affirmation. She had a strong soprano voice. With that firm introduction, I didn't feel like I had a choice in what she claimed she was going to be in my life. It was so unbelievable that Uncle Jimmy and I burst into laughter.

"I don't see what's funny. Here's my business card. Call me tomorrow," she said without cracking a smile and simply walked away.

She was fire. She left us burning in her flames as she hopped into her silver, 520 E Benz and sped off. I had no choice but to call her, Ms. Rennie---if you're nasty.

I didn't know much about the responsibilities of a publicist, so Uncle Jim broke it down for me.

"A publicist helps you get the attention of the newspapers, magazines, and so forth," Uncle Jim explained.

"So she's different from Mike?"

"Yeah," Uncle Jimmy said.

"If I want to do an interview on the radio or TV, Natasha hooks that up for me?"

"Exactly! She'll also help you create and maintain a positive image---"

"Even if I get in trouble?"

"Even if you get in trouble," Uncle Jimmy confirmed with a bowed head, lowered eyes and a cautious voice as if to say... *Don't you get in know trouble, boy!*

My parents continued to be my mediator for all things business related. I wasn't sealing the deal with Natasha without their approval. I called Natasha and she came to the house the very next day.

"First of all, Mr. and Mrs. Chaney, I'm a big fan your Tray's work."

Natasha looked at me out of the corner of her eyes.

"So you knew who I was from jump when we met?" I asked with a screeching, surprised voice. My eye brows were in position of shock.

"Of course I did! I knew you back when you were on Michel Wright's show." Natasha never turned her position away from my parents. I'm glad she didn't 'cause my brown skin was feeling beet red. I was embarrassed 'cause I didn't remember her from that moment.

Opening her leather briefcase, Natasha presented her buffet of services and prepared outline of events she wanted me to appear. She had already set up newspaper interviews. I was impressed with her professionalism and gusto. With her services came a price. Natasha was kind enough to break down her specific fees that were detailed in a contract prepared by her attorney. Natasha left no room for me to say, *Thanks, but I'm not interested.*

If there was any breathing room for another publicist to come in and take me as a client, I was sure Natasha had already sucked up the air between us. Natasha, like she said, was hired and became my publicist.

Before long, I was in newspapers, doing charity events, and making as many public appearances that Natasha could put her hands on. In her industry, Natasha became known as a psycho publicist. No was not a response Natasha was accustomed to hearing. She'd pound the pavement until she somehow constructed the letters to that resulted in her getting what she wants.

If Tray appeared in any paper as TREY, someone's ears at the paper would be on fire.

"You're not printing this with my client's name incorrect. That's just not going to work!" Natasha corrected some poor intern until management took care of it.

Even if we were just going out to eat, Natasha had two or three of my portfolios, *Just in case we run into someone who makes things happen.* I trusted my career in her hands. Why shouldn't I? After all, her client list included Jermaine Dupri of So So Def Records, Clinton Portis, Terrell Owens and a host of other heavy hitters. I was the first actor she represented, and that made me special.

SEASON THREE EPISODE FIVE
The Cuban and a Jeannie

The *Kitty of the City* (Meow), showed me much love. Jeannie Jones of Radio One's WKYS 93.9 FM has a voice that commands your attention. She has a spot on the station called *Jeannie's Juice*, where she gives listeners the latest in entertainment news.

Jeannie had often mentioned other characters that play on *The Wire* in her broadcast, but she didn't know me. Since I could bring a little local flavor to her segment, I used my resources to get in touch with her.

DJ Alizay always made the club jump when he was spinning the wheels of steel. In the past he showed me love on the mic as well as his partner in radio, Antonio "The Cuban Cigar Smoker." I met him while chillin' in Club VIP while expressing my interest in meeting Jeannie and getting on the air with her.

"Man, Jeannie will be here tonight!" Alizay said with excitement. "I'll introduce you to her."

Then a loud voice from no where was heard over the music.

"Que Pasa! Que Pasa!" a brother with arms outstretched was wearing a black and red 93.9 FM t-shirt shouted to me.

Before I could say anything, he asked Alizay, "Who is this little drug dealer from *The Wire*? Ain't you too young to be in here?"

I said, "Man I'm the life of this party. I may be young, but I'm fly!" I said with confidence. Antonio looked at me and cracked up laughing.

"I'm Antonio, "The Cuban Cigar Smoker.'"

"Oh my goodness, you the dude from the radio!" I said in amateur excitement.

"Duh! And you the dude from *The Wire*. Poot, right?"

After our initial introductions, we just kicked it and talked about me getting in good with Jeannie Jones. Both Alizay and Antonio were positive that Jeannie would take to me.

Until that time came, I had to show and prove my pimp game at the club. I was making good with the ladies---even the ones Antonio was after. He introduced me as his brother. That helped me even more.

This one lady in particular walked up to Antonio. She asked, "Who is this kid you have with you?"

I interrupted and said, "Wassup, sweetheart? I'm Tray Chaney. What's your name?

"Meow! I'm Jeannie Jones, baby, and I love you on *The Wire*.

WHAT AN INTRODUCTION! I was caught off guard. I couldn't believe I was getting fresh with Ms. Jones (perfect time to be formal, eh?).

"Jeannie, I am soooo sorry,"

"No need to apologize," she said with sincerity.

"I'm a fan of the work you do on KYS. I'm flattered to meet you.

Antonio and Alizay laughed me out. I was put on the spot. Jeannie was so beautiful that night too. She put the other women to shame in her fitted dress. She was hosting at the club that evening.

Even after the awkward first impression, Jeannie put me on the show that following Monday. It was an over the phone interview, but I was on nonetheless.

Lessons I learned at Club VIP:

- Don't pimp too hard. The very person you're trying to attract might be the one to increase your paycheck. Don't push the envelope.

- There is such a thing as being too cool in front of new friends. The warm air you'll feel will be from their laughter when you're caught out there with your pants down.

Mic Check. One Two. One Two. And I'm out.

SEASON FINALE
We Interrupt This Progam...

Do you remember those tears I had to fight to conjure up during a taping of *The Wire?* Apparently, they were pre-meditated. This is the part of the art I wish never came true.

I hadn't seen my best friend, Eric, in weeks. Talk around the neighborhood was that he had some new friends in D.C. I had never met any of these dudes. Funny thing is that when we were little, we made a promise that we would never gain new friends 'cause they couldn't be trusted like the ones we grew up with---Big Lou was an isolated incident.

Another friend, Tone, would go to the District when Eric kicked it there. So I didn't worry as much about Eric 'cause I knew Tone would not let anything to happen to him. Eric was our boy.

We all use to look out for Eric 'cause he was one of our friends that would talk a lot of trash to other guys and he wouldn't really fight them like we would. He merely brought on comic relief for us.

Eric did have a look that would scare you to death, though. On the exterior, Eric looked mean and hateful. He could talk like he would destroy you if you mess with any of us. Deep down, Eric was one of the meekest most humble guys in the neighborhood. Everyone who knew Eric, loved him. He would literally give you the shirt off his back.

Almost every one of our friends would go to Eric's house if they didn't want to go home. There were times when some of our boys needed money and Eric would pull out the dough to take care of his boy. We all use to borrow Eric's shoes, jackets or any dress clothes that we needed for any occasion. Eric's house was a one stop shop. His parents were cool too.

Eric's mom was the cornrow lady. The heads in the hood were always freshly braided. She didn't charge a lot, so she was okay with us. When we stopped noticing Eric around, his house was no longer the haven. It would seem a little weird rollin' up to his crib and he wasn't home. I was uneasy about his sudden disappearance 'cause he was my friend and it was strange for us not to keep in touch.

"Have you seen Eric?" Mom used to ask.

"Naw. He don't hang around here no more." That was my standard response. I really wish I had more to say.

I was asleep one night in my usual spot, the basement, when Mom shook me awake.

"Tray wake up! Look at the news! It's Eric, your friend," She was spastic.

I thought I was dreaming until I heard the television turned up as loud as it could go.

"The body found is that of 19 year-old Eric L. Hayes II. Hayes was abducted in the District and killed in Prince George's County," the reporter said.

I was sick. I jumped up and grabbed a blank videotape and put it in the VCR to record the other reports. I was in total shock, and I could not believe what I was seeing on the news or hearing. *Not my friend Eric,* I kept saying to myself. I couldn't cry. I didn't hug my mother. I was just numb all over.

I sat down in the basement for the rest of the morning rewinding and watching that tape---hoping the scene would change. Hoping, yet again, I was in the studio watching the pages of a scene unfold, and Eric would rise out the corner of that apartment where we shot him with blanks. I was in denial like a mug.

By 6AM, my phone rang and it was a collect call from Zeek. He was back in jail. It was very unusual for him to call my house at this time in the morning though.

"Tray, did you see the news?" Zeek asked

"Yeah, man. I'm watching it right now."

There was a moment of silence at that point in the conversation. There was nothing to say. What could we say really? Our boy was gone. Whatever we tried to say, there was sadness in our voices. Neither one of us cried or did anything at that time. I didn't want anyone to see my emotions, so I held it in.

After Zeek's time was up on the phone, everyone else started calling the house. Dudes I hadn't heard from in a while were blowing up the house phone. It wasn't a dream. It was reality. Eric was dead.

Who could have killed him? Why would they kill such a good man? Eric was MY best friend. Not that I wished it to be anyone else, but Eric? That just didn't sit well with me.

Around five or six o'clock that evening, Mom asked if I wanted to go over Eric's house---to pay my respects to his family. Even though I was a little scared, I went. I didn't want to see the sadness in their eyes either. There was so much history that I would feel crazy just standing in the door.

Chicago and Darell came by the crib. They asked if they could come with me. I needed the company---company that understood what I was dealing with. Just before we left, I had to take the trash out and feed and walk Shadow, our dog, before we headed to the Hayes' house. Mom stood at the front door watching me. She knew how hurt I was, but still refused to let her see me cry.

"Tray, baby, are you going to be okay?" Mom shouted from the door.

That was it. I broke down to my knees and cried as hard as I had ever cried in my life. My cousin Darell grabbed me and hugged me as tight. Chicago' burst of tears followed. We were done.

"Tray, I forgot about you man, I know that was your best friend and I didn't think to hug you or comfort you. I'm sorry, man." We all cried together.

The tears kept rolling out of eyes up to the time we reached Eric's house. Eric's father answered the door. As soon as Mr. Hayes saw us, he grabbed all of us like we were his sons.

"Ya'll were Eric's friends," he cried. "I tried to tell my son to stay off the streets and he didn't listen to me! He didn't listen. That's why he is not here today." Mr. Hayes let us go and looked us square in the eyes. "Please listen to your parents. They will never tell you anything wrong. Don't be in them streets getting into fights, selling drugs or doing anything that will jeopardize your lives! You hear me?"

"Yes, sir," we said in unison.

After Mr. Hayes finished talking to us, we all went in the house to speak to the rest of the family members. Everyone thanked us for coming and after that we left. As we drove back home, there was nothing but silence in the car. We sat around the rest of the night with our heads down feeling hurt, and then Darell spoke.

"I know whoever did this to Eric, didn't have to kill him.

He probably begged them not to kill him and they did it anyway.

Eric didn't deserve that," Darell said with frustration in his voice.

"I wonder if we know who did this. I hope it's not anyone who lives in this neighborhood. 'Cause if it is, we have to get them for this mess." I said shaking with fury.

I couldn't believe I was speaking violence from my heart. I meant it too. I knew, however, no matter what I did in retaliation would never bring Eric back.

A few days went by and it was time to go to the funeral. I had a bad attitude that entire day. I wasn't sure how I was going to handle the final moments of my best friend's life. I didn't know how I would react to seeing Eric lying dead in a casket. Just to be on the safe side, I asked Mom and my girlfriend, at the time, to accompany me. As I walked up to the church, I noticed a few dudes who shouldn't have been there. They were the same guys we use to beef with in the other neighborhoods. They didn't have respect for Eric, therefore they shouldn't have shown their faces. That's just how I felt.

As I sat in the church looking at Eric's casket, I couldn't cry anymore. I started thinking about all the fun times that we had together. We had some great times kickin' it back in the day. Taking this approach made me feel better. Then I noticed my cousin Darell walking in the church with this mug on his face. He walked by the casket, wiped a tear from his eye and walked back up the aisle. He didn't speak to anyone in the place except me and Mom. He kissed her on the cheek as to say, *I'm not being rude. This is just how I'm dealing right now.* He probably felt the same way I did when he saw our enemies at the church.

It was a good thing Eric's dad was a D.C. police lieutenant 'cause the cops were everywhere. They were there to support their fellow officer in his time of mourning. If the police weren't there, we probably would have had some words for our uninvited guests. There was too much hurt in the atmosphere and anything could have popped off.

I stayed at the funeral as long as I could. After seeing his family crying and Eric's girlfriend falling out in the middle of the aisle, I had to go. It was just too much for me.

I went home to get some rest, but all I kept thinking about was Eric in that casket wearing a Kufi on his head. I could actually see where they shot him. The image wouldn't leave my mind. I finally, decided to say a prayer and get some sleep.

When I woke up the next day, I got together with my friends and we sat around talking about Eric that whole day. Eric was our Cochise---like from *Cooley High.* It really was "so hard to say goodbye to yesterday."

We laughed and joked about the good times we had with Eric. After coming to our senses, we knew it was best to let the law handle the case instead of taking matters into our own hands. And justice was served. Eric's killers were caught, convicted, brought to trial and sentenced to life. One became the first to be sentenced to death in the state of Maryland.

It's amazing---the memories we accumulate to help us remain steadfast. What's even more amazing is the support system God sets up to carry you. I wanted to be carried onto the road of continued success---just not in a pine box.

To all you young men and women with aspirations beyond the norm, you have limitless opportunities. You have choices. You have the choice to do well, just get by or the choice to say goodbye to all the possibilities of life. Don't wait for opportunity to knock at the door, just open it and walk through the door. The best thing someone can tell you is no. That's when you start welding your own doors.

Eric, the next episodes of my life are made to carry on the dreams you never saw come true. Rest in peace, Eric and hello to the next generation of Tray Chaneys. Your past is the truth, but use it to make a better tomorrow. I'm starting with this little one I hold in my hand.

"Mr. Chaney, the baby needs his rest now."

ROLLING CREDITS

"You are worthy, our Lord and God, to receive glory and honor and power, for you created all things, and by your will they were created and have their being." -Revelation 4:11

I first have to thank Jehovah, God, for allowing this book to be written and for giving me the ability to write part of my life's story. He's the most high over the entire earth.

My warmest thanks and appreciation also goes to my mom, Mrs. Elaine L. Chaney. Thank you for inspiring me to write this book. Moms really do know best. Mom you're very encouraging and without you this life story would be a secret. Thanks for all that you have done. Much love, Mom.

I can't forget about my dad, Mr. Samuel Chaney, Jr. who has been a great support throughout the whole project. Thanks for being patient. I know you wanted this to happen more than anyone else. I also appreciate your generous donations in helping to get the ball rolling. Much love, Dad.

Thanks to my sweet sister, Candis O. Chaney, who was there to kick it with me and remind me of some of the events that took place in the book. You're the sister that every brother needs. Your smile and witty character is so hilarious. No one can compare to you. Maintain your happy personality and stay the way you are. I love you little sis.

I have to give a special thanks to my wife Mrs. Ayesha A. Chaney. You put up with me and took good care of our two beautiful children, Martina and Malachi, while I spent some of our quality time trying to get the book together. Your loving understanding and kindness are truly remarkable.

Thanks to my entire family for all of your support throughout my life. You have been an inspiration to me. Grandma Rosa Chaney, Granddad Samuel Chaney Sr., Aunt Maria (Peedie) for all your cooking, Aunt Marcia, Aunt Anita, Uncle Bernard, Aunt Kaye, Aunt Teressa, Uncle John, Uncle Jimmy and uncle Mark, thank you.

Cousins James, Darrell and Shawn, you three are not only my cousins, but you are my best friends. Thanks for being there through the thick of my life. You play a big part in this book. I couldn't tell it all, so we'll have to save some for later. Some events we'll just have to take to the grave---you know what I'm saying? Thanks for being my family.

Danny, Darnell and Marcus and the late Eric Hayes, you will always be my true friends. Marcus, a special thanks to you for the contributions that you donated towards this project. It really meant a lot to me.

Yolonda D. Coleman, thank you for collaborating with me on *The Truth You Can't BeTray.* Your gentle, kind persistence enabled all of this to come together. I know you stayed up late nights to make this happen for me. I truly appreciate you for all your hard work and for being interested in me enough to take on this project. I look forward in working with you in the future.

Thank you, Rhonda Henderson and Brianna Jones for being another set of eyes for revisions, Brandon Walker for creating my title, Kurojintu for coming in the eleventh hour to make the cover art meet the right specs. Greg Coleman, you were the middle man who got this project on its way. Thanks.

Also special thanks to Michel Wright from WPGC 95.5 for being the first radio personality to ever put me live on air. I love you to life. Yo my man Freaky Ty, u a wild boy! Keep holding it down. Flex, Rane, Shack-n-da-Pack, Donnie Simpson, Chris Paul and the dirtiest DJ alive Dirty Rico. To sum it up, I am thankful for the entire WPGC family. I LOVE YOU ALL.

To my promotional staff that helps me promote some of the hottest events in DC, thank you (My dawg Jean D. Fordre aka Jonathan Tate and 3rd Eye Entertainment). Wassup to Rasheed and Snails. To the hottest band ever to hit Washington, D.C., LISSEN the group. Scooby, I never heard anybody put a song together like you. You have a gift. Tuffy, my homey, you are crazy with the rappin', dude. You're one of the hottest in the game. O, man, I haven't forgotten about you. People are gonna be mad when my albumn drops 'cause you'll have a major credit on it. Along with Tuffy and Scooby, we're gonna shock the world.

Jeannie Jones *(the official kitty of the city)* you are just entirely too sexy. I love you to life for looking out for me on the radio by giving shout outs, interviews and just putting me on. You are true. To my people at 93.9 WKYS, Antonio "the Cuban Cigar Smoker," thanks man. Anything you said you would do you did. You always look out for me and make me feel like Denzel Washington when I walk into clubs. DJ Alizay, when are you going to teach me how to DJ? You know you're a bad boy on the 1s and 2s.

To the *The Wire* staff, David Simon, Nina Noble, the late great Robert Colesberry (Rest in Peace) and Ed Burns. I can't name the whole staff, but you know who you are. I love ya'll so much. You helped Tray Chaney rise in entertainment. To be apart of one of the hottest, critically acclaimed shows in history is huge. I also dedicate this book to you. Next I will be looking for you all to back me up on the movie for the book *(planting seeds)*.

To the entire cast *The Wire,* ya'll have taught me so much---especially the crew I started with. My man Larry Gilliard (D'Angelo Barksdale), Michael B. Jordan (Wallace) and of course JD Williams (Bodie). JD I know you heard this before, but dawg I follow your pattern with this acting business. Much love to you!

The best casting agency in the world Pat Moran and Associates. Pat I love you. You are responsible for the world knowing who I am. Pat I look forward to us one day auditioning people for *The Truth You Can't BeTray*, the movie (just planting seeds again).

Last but not least, to Malachi, my son. I can't wait until you're able to read this. You are the reason I live. I look forward to seeing your smile everyday. You are the only person on this earth who can make me shed tears just by looking at how beautiful and special you are to me. This book is going to be a huge part of your history, and it will be a huge part of your future. Trust me. I am just setting up the path for you to be even more spoiled, yeah I said it. I want you to want for nothing. You deserve it for just being born. I will always be the provider I am for you, your mother and your sister. Son, Daddy loves you. It's going to be a trip watching you grow up, but don't worry that will all be written in the next book. Now, that's a trip right there (lol).

To all the crews still having beef, it's not worth it. Life is too short. Squash it and move forward. Your future depends on it.

If I left anyone out, charge it to my head and not my heart. Anyone who feels slighted, call me out---lunch and dinner is on me when the book blows up. And I'm out!